ONE OF OUR LIONS IS MISSING

ONE OF OUR LIONS IS MISSING

Simon Baynes

ATHENA PRESS
LONDON

ONE OF OUR LIONS IS MISSING
Copyright © Simon Baynes 2006

All Rights Reserved

No part of this book may be reproduced in any form
by photocopying or by any electronic or mechanical means,
including information storage and retrieval systems,
without permission in writing from both the copyright
owner and the publisher of this book.

ISBN 1 84401 727 3

First Published 2006 by
ATHENA PRESS
Queen's House, 2 Holly Road
Twickenham TW1 4EG
United Kingdom

Printed for Athena Press

All men dream: but not equally. Those who dream
by night in the dusty recesses of their minds wake
in the day to find that it was vanity: but the dreamers
of the day are dangerous men, for they may act their
dreams with open eyes, to set the world afire.

> T E Lawrence, *The Seven Pillars of Wisdom* (1926)

The world had gone mad, and in many parts of Europe,
advertising your love of Jesus Christ was like painting
a bull's eye on the roof of your car.

> Dan Brown, *The Da Vinci Code* (2003)

CHAPTER 1

Amanda's bedside phone rang at 5.20 a.m. It was Harry, her boss.

'Get onto this quick,' he said. 'Now – it's big.'

She struggled to focus. What on earth could it be? A rail crash? Another terrorist attack? A suicide bomb? Nothing last night had given any warning of a story. London had been calm for months… But of course that was the way of terror – no warning.

She groped for paper and pencil: the instinctive journalist.

Monumental London lay sleeping under a bleak sky. Gusty wind drove the clouds over the city, rain showers swept the streets and now and then a fitful moon visited dark corners. Tributes to the long dead and long forgotten accepted their wintry fate. Only the caresses of the February wind touched their cold surfaces; only the attentions of pigeons briefly flattered their stony silence. They had no notion that tomorrow would be any different from their million yesterdays. No hint of festival surprised their habitual neglect.

The South Bank lion stared in magnificent aloofness across the river to the ceaseless drone of traffic over Westminster Bridge. To the west, Boadicea drove her chariot blindly onwards into the night. Outside the Palace of Westminster, Cromwell leaned upon his sword and the Burghers of Calais nodded their venerable heads. In Parliament Square iconic Churchill stared towards the chamber of the House, where his voice had thundered, and the mediaeval Westminster Hall where his body had lain in state.

Even in the small hours traffic still flowed around the Cenotaph in Whitehall, whitened now and then by the moon. King Charles I rode his bronze horse southward towards the old Banqueting Hall, his place of execution. Nelson looked down from his unassailable height, dreaming of Trafalgar two hundred years ago. Queen Victoria sat regally on her white and decorated plinth in front of Buckingham Palace, facing The Mall. Prince Albert, her dearly loved consort, stood aloof under his gigantic gothic canopy in Kensington Gardens opposite the Royal Albert Hall. The poet Byron in Hyde Park; Queen Anne on the forecourt of St Paul's Cathedral; Samuel Johnson outside St Clement Dane's Church in the Strand; Shakespeare in Leicester Square, dreaming of his world of fantasy, the insubstantial pageant of his own creation – all London's bronze and stony monuments stood in their centuries' sleep, little dreaming of any change, untroubled by thoughts of resurrection to a brighter day.

Amanda struggled into wakefulness, rubbing her eyes.

'Harry, what the hell? It's five in the morning. I was up till one.'

'OK, OK, but this is the big one. You're needed, now ASAP. I want you out there.'

And then, to flatter her into action, oblivious of sexist innuendo, he growled, 'You're our best man, so let's have you.'

Work came before everything. The chance of a scoop was Amanda's number one driving force. She staggered to the basin and plunged her face into cold water, forcing her mind to concentrate, gearing up for action. She was on the job.

CHAPTER 2

Yellow Wednesday, the press dubbed it. London had never been so yellow since the days of the great smog. There was no paint, no vandalism, no damage; nothing you could charge anyone for. Nothing that could be called graffiti: no words, no religious battle cries, no political slogans, no racial invective, no advertising, no obscenities. Only a tide of yellow that flowed from Aldgate to Notting Hill, from Bloomsbury to Lambeth. London rubbed its eyes that morning and woke to a world of persistent, ubiquitous, baffling, hilarious yellowness.

Amanda yawned. 5.20 a.m.

'Get on to this,' Harry was saying. 'Yellow. I don't care how you do it, but get out there quick. Look for anything yellow. Texts coming in from all over the place. As far as we know, it's confined to London. Drop everything else. Just get me news of anything yellow, and get it in fast. And pictures. Get Marcus. I'll be on my mobile all day.'

He gave her some details.

'Good luck. Go for it. This is big!'

Amanda struggled to shake off the feeling that the voice was the continuation of a dream. No, it was real. The phone had rung. It was Harry. She had the true reporter's nose and knew that she must be out on the streets. There was a story, bizarre though it sounded.

She fought off sleep, and in six minutes she was dressed, had some coffee on the go, and was gathering her needs for the day – watch, mobile, camera, notebook and pencil, money, cards, keys, make-up, comb, a bottle of Evian. The one-bed flat in Bethnal Green was lonely since her last boyfriend had moved out, but there was more space to spread her things and no one to disturb. She left the kitchen untidied, the bed tousled; every minute counted. Who would sleep in it next? She was always on the prowl.

She looked out of the window. It was still dark and drizzling. Then she gave a start. Among the cars parked nose to tail down the street was a bright yellow mini. Any other day she wouldn't have given it a thought. The illusion of being in a dream persisted.

She phoned Marcus, the cameraman. Marcus was plodding but efficient; not an exciting companion for a day's work, but reliable. He shared a decaying terraced house in West Ham with two friends and was wedded to his camera.

'You're needed now... Yes, now! Of course it's dark! You've got a flash, haven't you? Harry says it's big. Yellow. I'll explain when I see you. Meet me at six, or as soon after as you can make it... Where? How the hell do I know? Say Aldgate East Station. And make it quick. Bye. See you there.'

Amanda spent a couple of precious minutes in front of the mirror before locking the door and dashing downstairs.

Marcus, grumpy but resigned, tiptoed to the bathroom over the creaky floorboards, trying not to wake the others. A quick splash under the tap, a quick smack of the brush through his hair, a quick grab at some clothes. But, there was no sense of hurry about the assembling of his photographic equipment. Piece by piece he checked it all with professional efficiency, with loving care. No one likes having to get up at five-thirty in the morning, but if it was to take pictures, that made it worthwhile. And if it was the chance of a scoop, Marcus was your man. He was not interested in the paper as such but if he could produce better pictures than their rivals, or produce them quicker, there was no holding him. Even the prospect of working with the alluring Amanda did not excite him more than the sensuous touch of shutter and lens; in fact he found her pushy and self-centred.

They met and started on their surreal assignment. Within an hour they realised that Harry had not been exaggerating; London was swathed in yellow. All morning they trekked the city, sending in story after story, picture after picture. It was not difficult to find locations to photograph. Everyone was buzzing with the news. Through the City they went: Holborn, Bank, Charing Cross, the Strand, Piccadilly, the West End, Parliament Square. Wherever they travelled yellow insignia beckoned, a flamboyant protest against the February gloom. It had all happened in a single night. London was ablaze.

The Monument, Wren's Doric column, flaunted yellow streamers obviously intended to simulate the flames of the 1666 Great Fire of London. The equestrian statue of the Duke of Wellington fronting the Royal Exchange, flanked by the Bank of England and the Mansion House, was similarly adorned. Temple Bar, the historic Wren archway so long absent from the City but recently reinstated in Paternoster Square opposite St Paul's, had huge yellow rosettes hanging from its venerable gates, while nearby the naked shepherd of Elizabeth Frink's 'Paternoster' bronze sculpture, with his five sheep, was decently clad in yellow shorts. Leis of yellow paper flowers beautified the lions in Trafalgar Square; a long yellow carpet stretched in front of the Whitehall cenotaph; bright yellow plastic tape was woven into the railings outside Buckingham Palace, and a straggle of people beginning to gather there stared up at Queen Victoria's statue to see the Widow of Windsor crowned with a wreath of daffodils. To the West, where the Prince Consort stared stonily across to the Royal Albert Hall, a crate of fluffy yellow ducklings lay at his feet. Strings of gold-foil chocolate coins were hung from the door handles of the Bank of England; one of the gondolas of the London Eye was draped in yellow taffeta; festoons of yellow ribbon hung from the bow of Eros in Piccadilly Circus;

Boadicea soared over Westminster Bridge in a billowing yellow cloak. Net bags full of lemons hung from the doorknob of – where else? – St Clement's Church, Eastcheap, recalling the old song. A twelve-foot yellow square hung outside the Tate Modern, mecca of avant-guard artists. The recently installed memorial to 'Animals at War' in Park Lane – 'They had no choice' – had no choice but to be decked with yellow garlands. Yellow-painted oil drums stood on street corners; yellow bollards appeared in unlikely places; trees, statues, gates, railings, lamp-posts, door knobs and knockers flamed and fluttered in a meaningless show of yellowness defying the drab mundanity of a Wednesday morning.

At ten-thirty Amanda and Marcus took a brunch break, exhausted by miles of tramping, scribbling, phoning and camera work. They bought all the first edition papers and scanned them for coverage. Their own paper seemed to have the edge so far. There was a brief report in the stop press; they recognised Harry's style. They were glad to see no mention in any other paper. Their news and pictures would have to wait for the evening edition.

'What the hell's it all about?' Marcus dug his teeth into a toasted bacon sandwich with relish. 'There doesn't seem any clue. Is it political?'

'Massive surge by the Lib Dems?' mused Amanda, slicing a bagel. 'But why? There isn't any big issue on the table at the moment. No election in sight for two years, not even local elections. Why go to all this trouble?'

'Yellow... cowardice? An implication of cowardice directed at the government, or the PM? Remember those rosettes?' They recalled the huge yellow paper rosettes, like prizes at a horse show, attached to the railings in Downing Street. 'But what could the issue be? Have they been more cowardly than usual? Nothing comes to mind.'

'Obviously it's the lead-up to something. I expect

tomorrow we'll get some frumping slogan. It's bound to be commercial. Advertising the *Yellow Pages* probably, you'll see.'

They slogged around for another couple of hours, adding to their stock of reports and camera shots, but the job began to get monotonous and soon the borough cleaners moved in to remove the decorations. They rang contacts in outer London: there was no evidence of anything unusual. The plague of jaundice seemed to have infected only central London. They bought all the evening papers, as millions of others were doing, the front pages flaring with yellow, and admired their own work. They called in at the office before knocking off. Harry congratulated them.

Wednesday, 13 February remained in their memories for a long time as a joyful hiccup in the staid routine of the daily grind.

CHAPTER 3

The phenomenon had extraordinary, and contradictory, effects on London. It lightened the atmosphere like a fall of snow. It created a holiday mood. The city buzzed. People on the streets, in trains and buses, shops and offices, talked to each other as they never had before. And people laughed. The muse of comedy broke into the world of anti-money-laundering regulations, zero preference portfolio unit trusts and enforcement of any estate right or interest adverse to or in derogation of the title of the insured. And everywhere flew bizarre speculations on the meaning of the outburst of frivolity. A protest against the inner London congestion charge? The area roughly corresponded. A protest by would-be parkers at too many double yellow lines? A subtle campaign by the Automobile Association to press its advantage over its rivals? A medical students' rag?

So strange is the working of the human subconscious, it was noted that passengers on the Circle Line, ringing the area affected, the line coloured yellow on the Tube maps, greatly increased for the day. The romantic assumed it was a prelude to some fiesta arranged for Valentine's Day, which was the following day, and searched their memories for connections between eroticism and the colour yellow. Malvolio's stockings in *Twelfth Night*... The Yellow Books of the decadent 1890s... that country and western song about yellow ribbons... they all seemed remote.

'Commercial' was the mature view of the majority of world-weary city workers. It had to be an advertising stunt. Honey, sports cars, hard hats, eggs, canaries, oil seed rape, mustard, custard, chrysanthemums, bananas – incongruous images tumbled over each other in the metropolitan mind to explain the unexplainable. But for some it had a more sinister aspect.

The phrase 'yellow peril' lurked in the memory; a far-distant and long-forgotten episode in the collective subconscious: the threat of China. Now, more than a century on, could China be the issue? China had nukes; the sleeping dragon. Was there a massive threat looming in transcontinental politics? Warning of a new series of terrorist attacks? Terrorism, for the last decade, had been linked inseparably to the politics of the Middle East; could the focus be shifting eastwards? Could the inscrutable Chinese have some dark political agenda not previously perceived? A resurgence of militant Maoism?

But if so, why announce it beforehand so quirkily? Why advertise so frivolously? A petty sense of humour did not go hand in hand with imperialist ambitions. '*Un homme qui rit,*' said Marcus, smugly recalling the French of his university days, '*ne sera jamais dangereux.*' One could not imagine something so innocent, something that gave Londoners such ephemeral joy, coming out of a sinister political machine with global ambitions.

Nevertheless, the Home Office was rattled. They could take no chances. The Met was alerted and hundreds of extra uniforms drafted in from Thames Valley Police. Scotland Yard cancelled all leave. Danger spots were patrolled. The emergency services were on standby. For two weeks London was on high alert, and the public, with grim memories of the appalling atrocities of suicide bombs not long past, were edgy as well as amused. The atmosphere was a strange mixture of uneasiness, puzzlement and elation.

13 February ended with more drama. The enigma deepened. At 3.45 p.m. in the newspaper office Harry's phone rang, as it had been doing all day.

'Amanda?' Harry queried. He expected frequent calls from his blue-eyed girl.

'And who's Amanda?' The voice was unknown.

'Who is this?' asked Harry.

'You don't know me, and it doesn't matter,' growled the voice. 'This is a tip off. You'll be glad I rang. You're interested in the yellow phenomenon, right?'

Harry had to acknowledge he was interested.

'By this afternoon, a yellow letter will be delivered to the Prime Minister at no. 10 Downing Street.' The voice was precise, the accent neutral. 'We thought you would like to know.'

'Thanks', returned Harry, trying to inject some cynicism into his voice; smelling a scoop, yet fearing a hoax. 'So what is this letter about?'

'I can't tell you, but it's a yellow letter. Could be important, wouldn't you say? We hope the PM appreciates it.'

'Yes, well, thanks, but what's it all about, this yellow stunt? Perhaps you'd like to explain? I'll make it worth your while.'

The answer was surprising; a long, leisurely chuckle, followed by words in rich, mock-Shakespearean tones: 'my way of life is fallen into the sear, the yellow leaf. *Macbeth*, Act V Scene 3. Remember, no. 10 Downing Street, the afternoon post. Have a nice day. Goodbye.'

And before Harry could get another word in, the line went dead. He tried to trace the call, without success. He sat for some minutes, debating. Then he flipped the directory, picked up the phone and punched in a number. After a long delay a voice answered.

'Prime Minister's press office. How can I help you?'

Harry introduced himself and explained the tip-off. He put on an air of sincere concern for the PM's safety and well-being.

'I felt it my duty to warn you. Could you pass this on to the PM's secretary? It could be just a hoax, but it could be serious, even dangerous. I wonder if a suspicious letter has been received?'

The secretary in question could see no point in denying it; open government was the policy of the day.

'Yes. A large envelope with a printed address label and a Budleigh Salterton postmark has been received. A yellow envelope, you're right.'

Harry fished for more information. 'Right. I hope it's not dangerous – I am sure security have been careful. We are all rather on edge with this yellow business. No one seems to know what it's all about yet, but perhaps it has political implications? I wonder if you would like to make a statement for the press?'

'No.' The answer was firm. 'A yellow envelope has been received. Report it if you like. That is all we are prepared to say at this stage. No statement. Thank you for calling. Goodbye.'

'But you must have some ideas on what it's all about...' Harry persisted. But the phone rang off. 'Damn!' he muttered, and banged down the receiver.

At no. 10, security staff checked the envelope carefully before opening. Could it contain anthrax? Explosive material? It seemed quite thin. Sniffer dogs did their work. It seemed harmless. It was opened. Inside was a single sheet of yellow A4 cardboard, blank on both sides. This was minutely examined, without any result. It was then delivered to the PM, who stared at it for a long time, twiddling his pen.

CHAPTER 4

Cordelia Beckford was not the greatest designer of her generation. Colleagues in the interior decorating business thought her work undisciplined. It had a certain flair – sometimes a genuine touch of originality, a hit-and-miss randomness that tried the patience of her department manager. But everyone enjoyed working with her. She had such a happy personality that she was popular with both the male and female staff in the studios in Lambeth where she worked – a rare achievement. And Cordelia was beautiful.

All her male colleagues, including her boss, had flirted with her at one time or another and enjoyed the adventure, but had not got far. They knew there was a boyfriend, or partner, in the background called Malcolm, who was a borough engineer, though he did not live with her. He remained a shadowy figure, never appearing at the office, and Cordelia never opened up about him. The remarkable thing was that relationships were not soured as a result. She determined on being everyone's best friend, and succeeded. She loved life, loved her work, loved London, loved Malcolm, loved her friends, loved food, the countryside, painting, birdwatching, loved God and all the world. She was unquenchably optimistic, unsquashably serene.

Valentine's Day came: 14 February. Cordelia received cards and presents from all her colleagues – marks of genuine affection as well as frustrated passion. Her beauty was not destructive. The office benefited. The office wags had enjoyed themselves, mentally espousing this goddess who remained so tantalisingly unattainable. Their messages betrayed various levels of lewdness and poetic skill:

'Cordelia, won't you let me design your interior?'

'Be my love, Cordelia; I would love to feel yer, in my arms tonight.'

'Darling Cordy, you make me feel quite bawdy.'

'Kiss me, darling 'Delia; you are touchy-feelier than anyone else I know.'

'Be my Valentine, my lovely Cord; I'd like to get you on my drawing board.'

'Dear Cordelia, you and I are designed for each other.'

But Cordelia was no dumb blonde. To begin with, her hair was somewhat reddish – gold when sunlight struck it. For another, she was articulate. She managed to express herself without either the worn expletives that seemed such an essential element of modern speech – weak language, she called it – or the stuttering string of 'just', 'like', 'you know', 'if you like', 'I mean', 'in a sense', 'know wha' I mean?', 'at the end of the day' inanities of twenty-first century English.

Like everywhere else in London, the studios buzzed with speculation on the cause of the outburst of yellow and, like everywhere else, no one could offer any sensible explanation. The spring designs had already been decided, but the firm fleetingly wondered whether they should make yellow the dominant colour of their wallpapers and fabrics for the summer.

Cordelia's colleagues came up with every possible solution to the mystery. Everyone had their own theory and dismissed others as improbable. She herself had nothing in particular to suggest; all she contributed was some innocent-sounding appreciation.

'Cheers us all up! Just what we need, the best thing that could happen to London. The best February we've ever had. We've had nothing but gloom for the last year or two; everyone's bracing themselves for another bomb. Now this has happened. Something totally different, something innocent and happy. Thank God someone has a sense of humour and a bit of initiative!'

Her colleagues were more cynical.

"Delia, love, you are so naïve.'

'Pious platitudes, I'm afraid.'

'We don't all have your trust in human nature.'

'My dear Cordelia, isn't it time you started living in the real world?'

'Poor Cordy. Incurably happy. Put a bomb under her desk, and she would say, "Oh well, it needed tidying anyway".'

They enjoyed teasing her and went on arguing.

Across London feverish activity continued. Every police station hummed with debate, theories, supposed evidence, supposed links, the supposed significance of this or that, but no positive action. CCTV cameras were scanned and scanned again for any clues, but nothing suspicious could be found. It was evident that cameras near the relevant trouble spots – the police used the convenient phrase, though really no trouble had been caused to anyone – had been blanketed beforehand. Whoever was responsible had done a thorough job; it was obviously a well-planned and coordinated operation.

No further phenomena appeared: no outbreak of crime or vandalism, no terrorist attack, no advertising campaign. The mystery deepened. After two weeks the state of alert was relaxed, the police reverted to hunting cases of drug-dealing, street fighting, racial abuse, mobile phone theft and petty vandalism. The Prime Minister's secretary questioned the Post Office in Budleigh Salterton but got nowhere. The yellow envelope and card was examined by police detectives without result and put on file. The press milked the story dry and turned back to asylum seekers, company fraud and motorway expansion. Talk in pubs and clubs turned to other things. Life slotted back into the groove.

That year was a leap year; many people expected weird doings on 29 February, another rash of yellow mania, perhaps. The press were on the alert. But the day passed with disappointing normality. All over the country girls proposed marriage to sometimes unwilling suitors. Cordelia did not propose to Malcolm, because they were already engaged.

March came, the Chancellor prepared the budget, the City prepared its counter-attack, Oxford and Cambridge trained for the boat-race and jockeys for the Grand National. Nothing remarkable happened in London until the incident of the water.

CHAPTER 5

London gushes with water. The tidal River Thames flows through the city, spanned by twenty-five bridges between Hampton Court Palace and the Tower of London. The Grand Union Canal skirts the city to the north and its junction with the Paddington Basin is known as Little Venice, a marina housing a mass of narrow boats and motor launches by which Londoners escape at times for leisurely cruises into the level countryside of Hertfordshire. Lakes and ponds enhance the many parks. From a footbridge across the most central of these, in St James's Park, there are stunning views of both Buckingham Palace to the west and the government buildings of Whitehall to the east, framed by trees. The Serpentine is a long, curving lake in Hyde Park, with its lido where by tradition bathers swim on Christmas morning, whatever the weather. The shallow Round Pond in Kensington Gardens is the delight of children and model boat enthusiasts; Buckingham Palace has its own private lake, and the lake in Regent's Park is popular for boating.

A great city lives by water, for health, recreation and sheer necessity. London's man-made water systems were Malcolm's special concern and interest. As a borough engineer he knew the complex network of reservoirs, filter beds, pipes, taps and pumping stations that kept Londoners washed and watered. Domestic use and industry accounted for only part of the consumption; the public services required their supply, especially of course the fire service; leisure demanded more; dozens of swimming pools dotted the capital, and here and there were ornamental ponds, basins and fountains, all helping to keep London cool and pleasant throughout the year.

Malcolm understood these things. Water was his life. Half his working days were spent underground. The supply of clean water, and the disposal of dirty, was his job. He could have shown sightseers around the city's hidden network of highways and alleys below the surface as competently as a guide shepherding a group of tourists above.

If the parks and gardens of London were her lungs, then the waterways were her digestive system. Daily she imbibed and excreted millions of tons of water. From the filter beds on Ruislip Marshes to the great Thames Barrier on the estuary, built to control freak tides and forestall flooding, Malcolm knew how water behaved.

It was the end of March. Malcolm worked quietly at his desk, dreaming of the Easter break and the holiday he was planning with Cordelia. The borough engineer's office in Belgravia buzzed around him with talk about the purple water. One of his colleagues who lived in Paddington cycled to work through Hyde Park, and passing the Diana Princess of Wales Memorial Fountain had stopped and stared in disbelief; the oval ring of Cornish granite, its water flowing in two directions with miniature cascades and waterfalls running down into the reflecting pool, ran purple. The structure had been controversial ever since it was constructed in 2004; now here was trouble again. Crowds were gathering, and the area was cordoned off for police investigation. This was something new: the colour purple.

London's immediate reaction was panic; it must be a new form of terrorist attack. Bombs they had become used to, and had almost come to accept them stoically as a fact of modern life, but this was far more sinister. The government had always had nightmares about poison gas; this could be worse. A contaminated water supply would be a major catastrophe. Once again heads at the Home Office were racked. Special meetings were called, coordinating the

Water Board, the emergency services and transport chiefs. All kinds of evacuation plans were tabled. Meanwhile, the forensic chemists analysing the purple water found no trace of toxic material. Whatever had caused the coloration was as harmless as grape juice.

Amanda and Marcus were on the job again. All through the morning purple water gushed in unlikely places. All the evening papers ran pages of photos and stories.

Marcus was concerned to get the colour exactly right on his plates, and extra care was taken with the developing. This could make the front page. With fierce competition in the office, to get any picture printed was a success; to get one on the front page was a major triumph.

They pushed their way through the crowds to the edge of the fountains in Trafalgar Square. Part of the square was cordoned off, with scaffolding and hoardings around the base of Nelson's Column. Some maintenance work was going on. They stared at the shallow pools.

'What would you call that?' said Marcus, adjusting his lens. 'Yellow I can handle, but purple is a bit more subtle. You women are better on colours.'

'Magenta,' said Amanda, scribbling the word. Her pencil jotted down the bare facts – the look of the Square, the weather (still grey), the maintenance work, the crowds. Nothing was unusual except the gush of glorious purple shooting into the air and cascading into the twin cloverleaf-shaped pools. Two boys were paddling in the shallow water. Children were scooping it up in their hands, smelling it and trying to taste it.

'Look, Mum, Ribena!'

'Don't you dare!' shouted parents, panicking. 'That could be poisoned! Don't touch it, get away from that!'

Amanda interviewed some of the bystanders, only too happy to get into the papers. Responses were varied.

'Do you really think this water might be poisoned?'

'Dunno, but I'm not taking any chances.'
'What do think is behind it?'
'Dunno. Could be some political protest. Could be an advertising stunt.'
'Do you think this incident could be connected to Yellow Wednesday?'
'Dunno. Could be, but I don't see the point. No one owned up to that. It's a total mystery.'

Amanda sent in her report and they moved on. They searched for pools and basins, decorative water features, cascades and drinking fountains. When compared, there seemed to be slight variations of colour, but whether they were properly called violet, lilac, magenta or mauve, the word purple covered the lot. It seemed that wherever water flowed or gushed in public places, purple was the colour of the moment.

Scotland Yard went to work. Hasty warning signs were posted wherever water appeared and sites were cordoned off. Samples were brought in from every possible location; forensic chemists carried out exhaustive tests, but in every case the liquid was found to be innocuous. Statements were made to the press, reports were sent to the Home Secretary, who sighed with relief but scratched his head in puzzlement. Malcolm's department worked overtime and were called in to many consultations with the police and the Home Office. They could offer no clues.

Malcolm met his fiancée for a quick pub lunch in Vauxhall Bridge Road. Heads turned as the beautiful Cordelia entered. They ordered beer and sandwiches and sat down. They talked of the purple phenomenon briefly and shared the reaction of their respective offices, but they were more interested in planning their Easter break.

'Yes, Norfolk. I found this B & B, really cheap, near Hunstanton. I've booked two rooms. Middle of nowhere, we can explore The Wash.'

'Sounds a bit primitive.'

'Yes, well, we want to save every penny for the wedding. And we decided on birdwatching. And you can take your paints. Should be terrific in spring. Migration, geese, and so on. Miles of mudflats and saltmarshes...'

'Great. I really love a good mudflat.'

'There we are then. Brilliant. Disneyland next year, if you like!'

They discussed dates, times, travel, equipment. They would go by train and travel light. Malcolm rose to go.

'Must dash, we've got a rush job on.'

'A rush of water, I suppose?'

'That's right, a rush of purple water!' They both smiled.

'Do you ever not have a rush job on?'

'No, nor do you!'

'I may have rush jobs, but I don't rush. Let 'em wait.'

'OK, just don't get the sack. See you tomorrow.'

'Bye, darling. Love you.'

'Love you too. Don't marry anyone else, will you.'

Cordelia, going home after work, bought a late edition of the evening paper and found what she expected. Besides the flow of purple liquid in public places, there had been another incident at no.10, leaked to the press by a phone call. A parcel addressed to the PM had arrived, a rectangular box wrapped in purple paper. Security was immediately on high alert. The parcel was removed by the police and opened with extreme caution. The sniffer dogs were brought in. It contained an unmarked two-litre plastic bottle of purple liquid. Exhaustive tests carried out under sterile conditions proved that the contents consisted of nothing but the purest blackcurrant juice.

Cordelia caught a bus in to the West End to shop. Going up Regent Street she passed one of those extraordinary and now redundant survivals of Victorian philanthropy, a drinking fountain. Water gushed from a lion's mouth into a basin and below it into a trough where dogs occasionally lapped. The water was still faintly purple. Cordelia smiled.

Detective Chief Inspector Norman Prior lay up to the neck in purple water in his flat in Redcliffe Gardens, SW5. The bubbles lapped his chin. It had been a hard day but he was in buoyant mood. Only that afternoon he had heard the news of his promotion to Chief. It had been a long time coming, but now the years of patient work faded into the background. Nothing could dim the glory of a new title, a new authority, a new office. He was going to take his wife out to the Ritz to celebrate, deliberately choosing a place he would never have dreamed of entering before. Now he was enjoying a leisurely soak in the bath. It was only after sloshing in a generous dollop of his favourite Radox that he realised the irony of its colour. The frustration of an unsolved mystery only momentarily dimmed the beauty of his day.

CHAPTER 6

Amanda Griggs was hungry. She prowled the jungles of urban life like a hyena. She was hungry for success. Her career had become her passion, eating into her personality and distorting her values. The paper was the main thing, the story was all, climbing the ladder of promotion her chief goal. She would become an editor: nothing could take the place of that overriding aim. That was glory.

She was hungry for money. She had a fast lifestyle and expensive tastes. Every opportunity for overtime or moonlighting she seized without hesitation. She drove herself to long hours of work and was ruthless in her demand for expenses on the job. Her work colleagues and even Harry, her boss, were awed by her dedication but constantly irritated by her hyperactivity.

She was hungry for men. Passionate devotion to work did not lessen in any way the craving for a relationship, for physical intimacy, for ecstatic experience. She had a raw lust for life that constantly demanded satisfying. She kept herself fit and knew how to make the most of her looks. Since her early teens she had teased and tantalised a string of boys. They fell for her easily, but no relationship had lasted more than a few weeks. She seemed incapable of giving herself wholly to anyone, and her ingrained self-centeredness eventually repelled.

Though she never saw it in those terms, she was also hungry for love. Her hardness had developed early; her mother had died when she was three and a callous and promiscuous father was no help to her. Love to her was only a word; it meant no more than the easy philosophy of pop music, the fantasy of romantic films, the eroticism habitually portrayed in the media. The reality of it had never once come near her.

Purple water day had a strange effect on her. Strong colour seemed to act as a stimulant, an aphrodisiac. She enjoyed the experience and revelled in the search for words. Her language too was highly coloured. She had the tabloid style and knew how to glamorise a story without straying over the line into absolute falsehood. Her reports glowed with exotic prose. Harry lapped it up.

A day of trawling the water sites of central London had not tired her. She was not home till nearly seven, but was prepared for a night on the town. Marcus had plodded along, concerned with light and depth of focus, ambitious only to get the colour exactly right in each case. Marcus was a willing workhorse, not a companion for a night out. Harry had frequently flirted with her but had not got far. No one else in the office attracted her. She had had a brief affair with a boy younger than her, a junior in the foreign news section, but he too was ambitious and had moved on to a job with one of the major broadsheets. She would have to look for a man elsewhere.

She changed out of work clothes, showered, picked a revealing dress for the evening, gathered up her accessories and took a bus to Fleet Street.

'Ichabod, Ichabod, the glory is departed,' she might have lamented, if she had ever read the Bible, or '*Sic transit gloria mundi*,' if she had ever read the classics. Fleet Street, once the eponymous home of British journalism, was no more. The street, of course, remained, the western boundary of the City of London, with some undistinguished shops, pubs and restaurants, but for many it was hardly more than a bus route; a place to travel through; a name on the Monopoly board. The great national newspaper offices had long since moved east to the modern tower blocks of Canary Wharf on land reclaimed from old docks and warehouses on the river.

Here in Fleet Street Amanda found her favourite pub. She ordered a vodka and coke, picked up a tabloid – her own paper – from the rack, perched on a bar stool, consciously showing plenty of leg and a certain amount of bust, and waited for the trout to rise. She did not have long to wait. A wandering young male floated into her orbit, using the paper as his excuse to chat. Amanda eyed him casually and decided that he was not unattractive.

'Funny stuff, that,' said the boy, taking a pull at his Heineken. He pointed to the cover picture of the fountains in Trafalgar Square blushing purple. 'That purple water business. What on earth's happening?'

'Yes. Good pic, don't you think? I know the guy who took it.'

'Really? Friend of yours?'

'Not exactly. I work with him.'

'So you're a photographer?'

'Nope. Reporter.'

'Wow! You mean you actually write stuff that millions read?'

'Yep.' Amanda played it cool. She would let him make the running.

'Wow! You mean you write stuff like this?' He pointed to the front-page story.

'Yep. I wrote that.'

'Wow!'

'Have you read it?'

'Er, well, no, not yet, but I will. So what do you think this is all about? Do you have a theory?'

'I don't do theories. I do stories.'

'Yes, I see, that's your job. But you must have some ideas – privately, I mean. There was that yellow business last month. Did you write that up too? Do you think they're connected? What's behind it all? Is it an advertising stunt? By the way, I'm Geoff.'

He held out a hand.

'Amanda. Nice to meet you, Geoff.'

Amanda was somewhat tired of the whole business of the purple water, having discussed it endlessly in the office; all she was interested in were her reports and the chance of making a good impression on Harry. But for the sake of a night out she humoured her companion and strung him along. They talked and talked. He bought her another drink. They moved into the restaurant section and ordered a meal. Amanda turned on the charm. She knew exactly how to handle the evening, contriving that he should pick up the bill, and when she suggested going on to a nightclub he was well and truly hooked. By midnight he was only mildly drunk, but wholly under her spell. A taxi home to her flat in Bethnal Green together, an invitation to come in for a coffee and the callow youth was hers for the night. She kept a cool head and had no intention of being late for work the next day. He boasted to his mates afterwards that he had seduced this sexy journalist who wrote front-page articles in a national daily; the reality was that she had seduced him.

CHAPTER 7

Detective Chief Inspector Norman Prior sat at his desk in Scotland Yard staring at the orange he held in his hand. He was not about to eat it. He regarded it with extreme suspicion. It might, after all, contain a bomb. His staff, in the intervals of answering the phone and writing reports, were thinking about oranges too. Most of them had bright ideas to suggest, but no one dared to voice them. The problem of the orange was the number one business of the day.

It was 1 April. Clearly that had something to do with it, but was it purely a joke? If so, it was an elaborate and somewhat expensive one. All through the morning reports were coming in of more and more orange sightings. It was always whole oranges, though of various types and in various containers. A large basket on the steps of St Paul's Church, Covent Garden – like a gift to the theatrical world from Nell Gwyn; a shopping bag full of them hung on the elaborate brass door handles of Fortnum and Mason's, the posh food store in Piccadilly; a neat row stuck on the railings outside the Athenaeum Club; a pyramid arranged in front of Cleopatra's Needle on the Victoria Embankment; a small crate at the foot of Queen Anne's statue in front of St Paul's Cathedral; a cornucopia of oranges addressed to Lyon King-of-arms left at the gates of the College of Arms in Queen Victoria Street; a flotilla of loose oranges bobbing on the lake in St James's Park. Always oranges, of different shapes and sizes – with one exception.

The church of St Clement, Eastcheap, in King William Street, near the Monument, was completed by Sir Christopher Wren in 1687, twenty years after the Great Fire of London. Its fine panelling, organ case and magnificent carved pulpit are original, though the altar has been victorianised. It survived the blitz of Hitler's bombing raids in 1940. It is less well known than other Wren churches like St Bride's Fleet Street, St Mary le Bow, or St Stephen's Walbrook; not many of England's children have ever visited it, but they know it in song.

> Oranges and lemons
> Say the bells of St Clement's.

And on this 1 April, April Fool's Day, both oranges and lemons adorned the front doorstep of St Clement's, carefully arranged there overnight by an unseen hand.

Prior stared at the specimen on his desk. Of course forensics were working on a selection of the oranges, all labelled with the time and place where they were found. Inside each one they found nothing – that is, nothing but orange juice. Was somebody – or rather, a considerable gang – out to make fools of the police? If so, they were dangerously close to succeeding.

Prior himself was becoming the target of ridicule, and unless he could come up with an explanation, it could only get worse. He had been put on the case of the yellow phenomenon and of the purple water. Now it was oranges. He had totally failed to connect these colourful outbursts with anything that might interest the police; there was no increase in street crime, theft, burglary, racial tension, football violence or political activity. The facts were simple, but made no sense. The three incidents must surely be connected; he tried to see a pattern, but it was irregular. He listed the evidence:

it was confined to central London;

it was widespread, so must be perpetrated by a large group of people;

the incidents all happened at night;

all involved colour;

all were harmless;

the Prime Minister had received wordless messages;

the incidents had happened in successive months, but unevenly spaced – mid-February, the end of March, 1 April.

That was all. But it certainly seemed like some kind of joke, and had ended on 1 April. Presumably it was the lead-up to some gigantic hoax that would occur today, but what was the point? There must be some political purpose, or why involve the PM?

Orange in politics meant one thing; it was the name of an ancient principality on the River Rhone, from which descended a certain William, who by the anti-Catholic machinations of the establishment at the end of the seventeenth century became King William III of the United Kingdom. Prior may have forgotten his school history, but like everyone else he knew that William of Orange had established Protestantism in Northern Ireland and the grateful Irish Presbyterians had perpetuated the name. It was they who, with their Orange marches and demonstrations, for most of Prior's lifetime had been a thorn in the flesh of the Catholic Sinn Fein Party and its associated Irish Republican Army. But as a solution to the problem that line of thought led nowhere. The Orangemen were passionate, intransigent, doctrinaire; religious fervour spilled over into political protest; they were articulate, vehement and voluble; they were ready to oppose violence with violence. But in the public perception at least, a sense of humour was one quality that was conspicuously absent in their make-up. If every orange planted on the London streets contained a miniature hand-grenade, the men of Ulster might have been the prime suspects: but every orange examined was as innocent as the ones in the nursery rhyme.

So was it an advertising campaign? The Orange telecommunications company was a natural suspect. The mobile phone industry was big business. Everyone knew the slogan, pasted all over the country, 'the future's bright, the future's Orange'. But big business did not go in for such quirky and haphazard methods of publicity. And even if it did, why the yellow and purple phases?

The only positive thing Prior could do was to ring no. 10 and warn them about the oranges and to alert all police stations. No. 10 was already on standby.

Sure enough, a parcel arrived. A substantial box wrapped in orange paper. Again, it was opened under conditions of tight security. A bomb disposal expert was on hand. No prints could be found on the box. Inside – a batch of the best Seville oranges. Each one was painstakingly analysed; every one was clean.

Cordelia invited Malcolm round for a leisurely Saturday breakfast to discuss holiday and wedding plans, and Malcolm smiled as he saw on the kitchen table a large bowl of oranges. 'Remember, oranges are not the only fruit,' he murmured mysteriously as he kissed her ear.

The capital was on the alert once again. The media hummed, Harry fussed and chivvied, Amanda and Marcus trudged the City and the West End. For many, even such an innocent and beautiful thing as an orange looked like a sinister threat.

Londoners were the victims of terrorist attacks, and ever since 7 July 2005 they had walked with a glance over the shoulder. They had become the target of ruthless killers, joining the people of New York and Washington, Bali and Madrid.

Prior remained under a cloud of gloom.

But stoicism won over fear. Daily life went on. The public faced life with earthy common sense, and in spite of the tension they were prepared to enjoy a little mystery, a diversion from the daily grind. Again they buzzed with speculation and the city was pervaded with a relaxed and happy atmosphere. The combination of oranges, April Fool's Day, the prospect of Easter holidays and some spring sunshine lifted the mood of the grey streets. There was laughter in Piccadilly and a nightingale sang, metaphorically at least, in Berkeley Square.

CHAPTER 8

The holiday mood pervaded even the studiously professional offices of Scotland Yard. While the burden of responsibility weighed more and more heavily on Prior, officers not directly concerned were enjoying the bonanza, and the whole atmosphere was lightened. Sergeant Hicks, Prior's right hand man, was enjoying himself. He was spending time on the case, and giving it all his thoughts. It was a break from routine, and he sniffed promotion.

'Chief,' said Hicks, acknowledging his superior, 'just got the reports from forensics on those oranges. Total blank. Nothing suspicious, apparently. What do we do next?'

'What would you do, sunshine?' growled Prior. 'Put yourself in my shoes. Any bright ideas?'

'Well, one thing did occur to me, Chief. I expect you've thought of it too…'

'Go on.'

'Well, colours of the rainbow. You know, violet, indigo, blue…'

'Where's the sense in that?'

'Well, Chief, we've had three incidents that seem to be linked. All colours, right? Purple: well, that could be violet. Or indigo. Not sure what indigo is. Or maybe the purple covers both. Then we've had yellow, and orange. Three colours of the rainbow. I bet they're going through the whole spectrum. I mean, there must be some point to it, so we can expect three more colour days; we've got red, blue and green to come.'

'Oh brilliant, Hicks. That solves the whole problem. There's just one little flaw. If you were going through the rainbow, for some bizarre reason, wouldn't you do it in order? You'd either start with violet or red. And what's the flaming point, anyway?'

'You're right there, Chief.' Hicks was not totally deflated. 'Just a thought that occurred to me. But if we do get another colour incident, I'll bet it's one of those three. And then we can be pretty certain there'll be two more to follow.'

'A pretty safe bet, wouldn't you say? I mean, there aren't any more colours, unless you go for black and white.'

'I don't know, sir. There's pink... and cream... and brown... and silver and gold...'

'Joseph and his flummocking technicolour dreamcoat! Get out, Hicks, and get some work done!'

'Yes, sir. But, wow, that's quite a thought. Joseph... I never thought of that...'

'Out.'

'Sir.'

What puzzled Prior most of all was the spacing. It was one a month – just; but nearly six weeks between incident one and two, only four days between two and three. That didn't make sense. And the colours; there must be some meaning. Political parties... football teams... racial groups... religious nutters... immigrants... asylum seekers... loony protesters – anti-hunt, anti-pollution, anti-development, anti-vivisection... He went through every current political, religious and social issue in his mind and could not find one to account for the irrational pasting of colour across the streets of London.

The evidence was filed and put on the back shelf.

CHAPTER 9

The Easter holiday arrived. Malcolm and Cordelia were two hours away from London: a world away. They arrived at a little village near Hunstanton and checked in to a tiny reed-thatched inn with only five or six bedrooms, at the end of a long, somewhat muddy lane. It stood on the edge of a river estuary, the East Anglian fenland stretching in all directions. A few scattered trees and houses dotted the landscape, a landscape whose flatness would repel any painter who was not interested in clouds. Spirits of the past inhabited the land: Constable, Morland, Crome. The quiet was palpable.

Mrs Cartwright, ensconced behind the bar that doubled as a reception desk, welcomed them warmly.

'I hope you'll like the room. Up the stairs and first on the right. It's small, but it has a nice view looking over the river and out to sea. And the bathroom's right next door.'

Malcolm glanced at Cordelia with the faintest beginning of a smile that only she would have noticed.

'Thank you, it sounds delightful. And the other room?'

Mrs Cartwright looks nonplussed.

'You wanted two rooms?'

'Well, that's what we booked. I did ask for two rooms on the phone, you remember?'

'I see.' She fumbled through a well-thumbed engagement diary. 'You're expecting someone else, then?'

'No, no, it's just the two of us, but we asked for separate rooms.'

'Separate rooms? Just for the two of you? I see. Well, I think we can arrange that, we're not usually full at this time of year. So you would like two single rooms?'

Cordelia smiled sweetly. 'Two single rooms would be

marvellous, if you have them. We're not married, you see.'

Mrs Cartwright experienced a mild shock of surprise, but it was good news in a small way: two rooms would mean a little extra cash. And here was a couple – at least they looked like a couple; two good-looking young people – wanting separate rooms. It would have been the norm in her young days, but now... She smiled broadly.

'Certainly. It's quite unusual these days, but if that's what you'd like, we can fit you in. But I'm afraid the second room will be very small, an attic, really. I hope you don't mind. Well, well, separate rooms!' She made an entry in the book.

'We're engaged,' said Cordelia, with a disarming smile, which won over Mrs Cartwright completely. It took her back to her courting days, in the nineteen-fifties, when things were done differently. She chatted happily as she mounted the crooked stairs to show them the rooms; chatted of the weather; of the dwindling local industries of fishing, boat-building, farming, reed thatching; of the river and the tides; of the birds that they had come to see.

'You'll not be wanting keys, I hope? We don't keep keys here.' She had heard that in town hotels every bedroom had a key. To the engaged pair, having no key seemed to set the seal on the kind of holiday they wanted. Malcolm had chosen well. They settled in. The peace closed in around them.

The weather was dull and chilly, with a touch of east in the wind, but they had not gone to sunbathe. For six days they tramped the coast, exploring creeks and rivers, wading through marshes, rowing in flat-bottomed boats, sleeping late, eating well, sampling the local pubs. For six days they never set foot in a car. When it was not too windy, Cordelia painted. Her style was unique, her line erratic, her use of colour vibrant and powerful. Her paintings teased and puzzled the viewer, but every one brought with it an uprush of strange joy.

The birds were magnificent. Arrowheads of geese marked the vast empty skies, gulls screamed and swooped, varied with more delicate tern. Dunlin and oyster-catcher at the tide's edge, widgeon and pintail on the salt lakes, snipe and heron in the marshes, were their daily companions. Was that a ruff? Binoculars and bird books came into play. An avocet? A bar-tailed godwit? They listened in vain for the boom of a bittern, but found reed and sedge warblers beginning to nest. The great bustard eluded them. Scaup and smew failed to show. The long-billed dowitcher would have to wait till another time.

They lived blissfully in the present. Work, the news, London, faded to dimness. Their only future thoughts were of the wedding, which was planned for July. And it was their common mind about the wedding that sealed their partnership and established absolutely the conviction that they were meant for each other. On a topic that is normally an endless source of argument and friction among couples, they were in total agreement.

'Let me not to the marriage of true minds admit impediment,' quoted Malcolm, from the sonnet now firmly established in the repertoire of wedding readings.

'Fine, I won't,' Cordelia smiled. 'Only we won't have that as a reading, it's been done to death.' And Malcolm agreed.

It was indeed a marriage of true minds. To every idea one partner put forward, the other agreed.

'It's got to be different, it's got to be real.'

'It must be in the open air. It'll be a witness.'

'Lots of colour, lots of music. Hymns that people really like. Lots of flowers.'

'We'll ask Antony to take it, Antony Kilbride.'

'Prayer, yes, but not read out of a book. Real prayer. Antony will do it, for one. He's got the gift.'

'Low budget. No need to spend thousands.'

'Dress simple. No need for anything elaborate.'

'Just plenty of good nosh! A stand-up buffet, finger food.'

'I'll make the cake myself.'

'No set speeches, just a time for anyone to speak off the cuff.'

'No cars, we won't need them. We can arrive and leave by train.'

'We'll make it fun for children. Toys, sweets, balloons, bubbles, party poppers...'

'No formal guest list, any of our friends will be welcome.'

'No distinction between service and reception, they can just flow together.'

Their wedding was certainly going to be different.

Easter came and they watched the dawn break over the North Sea. The sun rose as if for the first time since the creation of the world. Flights of mallard rose with it, painting the sky with glory. Nothing could spoil the magnificence of the level sea and the level land, mirroring tumultuous clouds and the streaks of colour in the east.

Norfolk bound them together as never before. As Malcolm photographed and studied the birds, as Cordelia painted, creation and creativity met. Love drew them closer, as if they were in touch with the very source of love. Cosmos and microcosm, the universe and the heart, beat in unison. Every embrace, every kiss, was a sacrament that mirrored and expressed a larger world. The evening and the morning was the sixth day, and God saw that it was good.

The holiday ended, the train carried them back to London and universal greyness enveloped them at Liverpool Street Station. April passed.

CHAPTER 10

'London's Red-Letter Day' ran the headline. So barren was the imagination of news editors that most of the front pages said the same. Only one or two tried variations: 'Vandals Paint The Town Red', 'Residents See Red', 'London Keeps The Red Flag Flying'. The search for puns was a daily journalistic chore.

'So Hicks was right,' Prior acknowledged to himself grudgingly. 'So we're going through the rainbow. But in a funny order. And they've kept the monthly pattern. Feb, March, April, May...' And then – 'My God, it's 1 May, May Day! So it *is* political. The Red Flag! But is it the same people doing it? And if so, why all the other colours?' And he scratched his head, coming up with the same masterly conclusion that he had expressed again and again over the past three months: 'It doesn't make sense.'

'So I was right!' said Hicks triumphantly, but not to Prior. 'It's the rainbow. Blue and green to go, and/or indigo, whatever that is. Just wait and see!'

Red-letter day consisted, literally, of red letters. By mid-morning the Post Office had delivered hundreds of red envelopes to addresses in central London, but only in very selected streets. The first reports came in from residents of Redburn Street, Chelsea.

Within an hour it was confirmed that every house in the street had received an identical letter – if you could call it that; a standard sized small bright red envelope, with a correctly typed name and address label, containing a single sheet of plain, unmarked paper, of the same shade of red. Nothing else.

Prior phoned the British Communist Party; they knew

nothing about it. They would hardly make a gesture and then not own up to it, so Prior accepted it at face value. If it wasn't political, what else could it be? Red... red... red... He racked his memory for any possible meaning of the colour red. Red light district was the only one that came to mind, but there was no reason to think that Redburn Street, Chelsea, was more depraved than anywhere else. The scarlet letter... but that meant letter of the alphabet. A red rag to a bull... it was certainly that, and he was the bull.

Amanda was busy again, knocking on doors, interviewing householders, phoning in reports. Marcus shot a few pictures, but after the first dozen the sameness of the story showed that more would be a waste of time, so he moved on to another job.

When Prior's office in Scotland Yard received a call from Redchurch Street, Bethnal Green, near where a May Day rally was going on, to say that similar red letters had been received, he wondered again if there was a political slant to the whole thing; but it was also becoming clear that the red letters were being sent to streets with 'red' in their name. Red Lion Square, near the British Museum, was the next to report deliveries, at which point Prior reached for the London A–Z map, scanned the street index and found a hundred and fifty-one entries beginning with Red. He let out a snort of frustration. However, by the end of the day it appeared that the deliveries were not widespread. Redhill Street, near the Cumberland Gate of Regent's Park, was the only other street affected. Prior pondered these four.

'Excuse me, sir.' Sergeant Hicks, ever the bright spark, was at his door.

'Yes, Hicks?'

'Well, Chief, just one thing occurred to me. The red letters. Only four streets, right? Red letters to red streets. It's just that the placing could be significant: Redhill Street, NW1; Redburn Street, SW3; Redchurch Street, E1; Red

44

Lion Square, WC1. Something of a pattern, wouldn't you say? north, south, east, west. Only a small thing, but could be significant, I thought…'

'Thank you, Hicks. I'll make a note of it. Anything else?'

'No, sir. Not at the moment.'

'Right.'

Prior then went through the wearisome procedure of warning the PM's office. It was becoming something of a routine. True to form, the PM received his red letter, which was minutely examined but found to be no different from all the rest. It contained no message at all.

1 May was a normal working day for Cordelia and Malcolm, as for most people. After work they met for dinner at a restaurant in Victoria, devouring the evening papers and taking great interest in the red letter stories before going on to wedding talk.

'I've got my list here. Quite a lot of them. All these cousins. And lots of them have small children, we'll have to have them too. How many on your side?'

They compared lists, discussed, prioritised; planned the music, food and drink, cake, speeches.

'No speeches, we agreed on that,' said Cordelia firmly. 'The usual thing is a farce: bride's father trying to be a stand-up comic and the best man trying to be as bawdy as he dares. It's painful.'

'It's true, the average wedding is so artificial, everyone pretending to be what they're not. Your dad may not like it, of course…'

'I'll square him. Much better that way.'

'And I don't need a best man at all. It's really a meaningless custom. Are you having a hen party?'

'I most certainly am not. I have plenty of friends, and we party a lot. There's no need to make fools of ourselves. And they'll still be my friends after 23 July. Stag party?'

'Ditto ditto. I hate stag parties. Never go to 'em.'

The same conversation went on year by year between engaged couples everywhere, but with rather different conclusions, while their parents discussed the same points and came up with their own ideas. Weddings divided families rather than united them; brides' mothers live in a state of nervous tension for weeks. Malcolm and Cordelia's parents had accepted long ago that they were both strong-minded and unconventional, and it did no good to argue with them. This wedding was certainly going to be different, and they accepted that.

Malcolm finished his coffee and paid the bill. They went out into the twilight. The sun tried hard to do what all Tudor poets expected it to do on May Day, and added a reluctant touch of redness to the evening sky. They walked to Victoria Station. The late edition papers were still displaying pictures of surprised and indignant householders holding red envelopes and the street names of Red Lion Square and the rest. Malcolm showed no particular interest. Cordelia smiled an enigmatic smile. Colour was her business. They parted with a long, luxurious kiss.

'Love is not love which alters when it alteration finds,' Malcolm whispered in her ear.

'O no, it is an ever-fixed mark,' she breathed, touching him on the nose. She dived into the Underground. Malcolm caught a bus.

Prior went home to his flat in Redcliffe Gardens and felt quite cheated that he had received no scarlet missive in the post.

CHAPTER 11

'Seven–four. Nice shot, Rev,' said Antony's friend, panting. 'Your serve.'

The squash court resounded with the whack of balls on racquets, balls on walls.

The Reverend Antony Kilbride liked to keep himself fit, and he was aiming to take part in the London Marathon next year. He was in his late twenties, but looked even younger; single, but a lure for any woman, with the body and features of a film star.

He was trying to persuade his opponent, an athletic young Pakistani bank clerk, to go for the Marathon too.

He was one of the privileged few among the clergy who worked in the inner city, and as such his ministry was peculiar. The dozens of Wren churches, and the few which pre-dated the Great Fire, had been built to serve the teeming residents of inner London. With the coming of the railways the population had moved to the suburbs, creating the doughnut phenomenon. The churches remained, except for those bombed in World War II, but with no residents to serve. Antony therefore found his ministry pointing in three main directions, apart from the occasional wedding or funeral.

First, the classic building lent itself to concerts, organ recitals, art exhibitions and other cultural events on weekdays – a significant part of the many kinds of free entertainment that London provides.

In sharp contrast was the ministry to the homeless. Down-and-outs, drop-outs, tramps, hippies, alcoholics and drug addicts all found their way to the side door and were glad of a place to wash and help with food and clothing. Antony threw himself into this work, as so many in the history of the city churches had done, and over a period got to know the regulars and become their friend. The creed to which he had given his life, the message of a loving creator, a compassionate saviour, seemed impossibly distant at first to the people of the streets who came in after years of hopeless loneliness, but time and persistent caring made a dint in their broken lives.

But thirdly, he found increasingly, in partnership with a team of dedicated leaders in the area, he was being called also to a ministry to the rich. His church was in the heart of the City, surrounded by financial institutions. His parish was taken up with banking, insurance, investment and trading. It was a mecca for international business. The Bank of England was three minutes' walk away and the Stock Exchange round the corner. Massive Victorian buildings jostled with contemporary thirty-storey steel and plate-glass tower blocks. But in them worked people, and people needed a gospel. In Antony's view, the gospel for the rich began with a challenge. A listening ear and a compassionate heart were as important to the affluent as to the homeless, but first they needed to be jolted out of complacency, the easy assumption that wealth was the primary goal, and the hollowness of a life turned wholly in upon itself. Antony was a crusader, an evangelist.

His convictions led him to cooperate with a growing movement in the City that sought to offer office workers a hand of friendship, an oasis in the turmoil of the working day, and at the same the challenge of a gospel demanding a personal response. But Antony differed from many earnest campaigners against materialism in his wholehearted enjoyment of life. People knew him for his incurable sense of fun and his sometimes zany humour. Strange to say, he was an admirer of the old Puritans, but his whole life was a protest against all that was meant by the word 'puritan' as it is popularly misconceived.

In the last year or two, Antony's energies had found a new focus and a new challenge. Several of the banks and institutions in his parish belonged to the oil-rich states of the Middle East. More and more the presence of Muslims was becoming a significant factor in the make-up of this most cosmopolitan of cities. Antony agonised like everyone else over the growing phenomenon of Islamic extremism; he prayed long and hard about it, but unlike many others, he took action. His church became a talking shop for Muslims and Christians. He kept a firm hand on the discussions, which were sometimes tense, but it paid off. Even with deep differences of ideology unresolved, people from both sides of the fence became friends. That, he thought, was a vital first step.

Antony and his partner finished their game of squash and went for a shower. Antony emerged refreshed and, having dried himself, switched on his mobile and opened a pocket diary.

'Malcolm? Hi, how are you doing? We need to meet some time to talk about the wedding, and – other things! When can you make it?... Thursday next week? Sorry, we've got a band practise... Yes, I play in this rock band. You didn't know? Come and hear us some time. Friday? That looks good. Say eight-thirty? Fine. Come round to my place. You know where?... Yes, it's right behind the church. See you then. Take care, love to Cordelia.'

He rang off and made a note in his diary. A wedding was a happy break in routine and he looked forward to Saturday 23 July with relish. Malcolm and Cordelia had become personal friends over the last few months. It was going to be a very special day and it appealed to his sense of adventure.

CHAPTER 12

Cordelia was working late. A boutique in Chelsea was doing a makeover and the job had been given to her. Deadline: the end of May. When total concentration was needed it was better to be alone. The rest of the staff had left the studio, which was perched on the top floor of an ancient building in Lambeth Walk. Cars and buses roared below. Commuter-packed trains rumbled past, running out of Waterloo Station. She was tired and the ceaseless flow of traffic mingled in her mind with the lines and colours on the drawing board with mesmerising effect. The incidents of recent months – yellow Wednesday, the purple water, the oranges, red letter day – swam round her consciousness, and it was hard to disentangle them from the job in hand. Design was her business, line and space her medium, light and colour her tools.

But Cordelia was thinking not of laminated flooring and curtain fabrics, pine panelling and counter space, but of marriage. And she was thinking not, as all brides do, of her wedding, now two months away, but of marriage itself, which many brides do not.

The strangeness of it, the rightness of it; the built-in inevitability of this unique but universal partnership, built into the fabric of creation, woven into the nature of human character.

Marriage. She considered the alternatives: permanent singleness, celibacy, promiscuity, divorce and remarriage, polygamy, a three-cornered relationship, single parenthood, same-sex partnership, communal life. All had been tried; people experimented with every form of human lifestyle, but these alternatives remained, in her mind, experiments.

No other way of life, it seemed to her, had that foundational Adam-and-Eve quality of universality and permanence that marriage had. It was, she believed, the way we are made.

Yet what a risk it was, what a gamble, what a plunge in the dark! Cordelia's daydream led her into strange trains of thought. Imagine two delicate and sophisticated electronic devices, each with its own inbuilt mechanisms and responses, complex and sensitive. Marriage was like trying to connect them (her eye fell on the mass of tangled wires behind her desk-top computer), and expecting them not only to work in harmony, but to work better: to achieve their full potential. It was like plugging them into a source of power outside them both, on which they would both depend for life. What endless possibilities for things to go wrong! Love was, she dared to believe, stronger than death; the greatest thing, the ultimate solution. But what a delicate instrument, vulnerable at every point.

Certainty and doubt coexisted in her thoughts. So Magellan must have thought, perhaps: the world is round; I will get back to where I started – but what if I am wrong? So Galileo: the earth does move around the sun – but what if I am wrong?

And so, Cordelia concluded, it is not a leap in the dark, but a leap of *faith*. And faith in action is trust; the trust of the swimmer who believes in water; the parachutist who believes in air.

And in that act of trust was the joy that gave meaning to everything. It was almost a physical letting go, as with all the sports that depended on the physical laws of nature, the cooperation with air and wind and water.

In her dreamy state Cordelia surrendered herself mentally to the action of abandonment, of skiing, diving, surfing, hang-gliding. The giving of oneself was the only hope of salvation, the only way to joy, the only path to reality. That was marriage, and she was ready for the plunge…

Brring-brring, brring-brring!

The telephone broke into her reverie. She let it ring; the office was closed. The answering machine clicked on and a message was recorded. But it rudely reminded Cordelia of the job in hand. She got back to work, concerned now with the coupling of primary colours, the pairing of wallpaper textures and curtain fabrics, the marriage of wood and steel. She made some progress before knocking off at 8 p.m.; tidied her desk, turned off the lights, locked up the studio and went downstairs to find something to eat.

CHAPTER 13

If Hicks was right with his rainbow theory – and Prior admitted grudgingly that he probably was – if Hicks was right, not that his theory solved anything, then they could expect a rash of green or blue in the next few weeks. So far the attacks had been one a month, though spaced so irregularly that that might have been a coincidence.

But certainly from 1 June Prior's sense of expectancy rose and he waited for reports of bizarre behaviour to come in. They were no nearer finding the perpetrators and still had no clue to their motive. If only they could catch at least one of the vandals, he thought, they could make a mighty example of him (or her), even if the only charge they could bring was causing a public nuisance or wasting police time – in his eyes, a very serious offence.

The days of June ticked by. The weather slowly improved, the grass got greener and the sky bluer, and Prior wondered if that was the only show of blue or green they were going to see. But, ever cautious about the possibility of serious public disturbance, he grew restless as the Queen's Official Birthday approached. Maybe the lunatics were planning some climactic outrage, and he could not relax. The enemies of Britain were everywhere; anti-monarchy feeling was growing. After all, if you hated a nation, it made sense to target the symbols of that nation.

Prior went to watch the rehearsal of the Trooping of the Colour parade, trying to imagine what a publicity-seeking delinquent would plan in order to make a splash. His imagination failed; all he could do was to urge the Met to tighten security for the event as far as resources allowed, keeping a reasonable balance of cover for the rest of London. He would look a proper fool if men were diverted unnecessarily while the crazy gang (as he mentally labelled them) had a field day somewhere totally different.

The day came. Prior was on edge. He kept making needless phone calls, fussing and fidgeting at his desk, watching the parade at intervals on a screen in the corner of his office, planning a response should any reports come in. Was someone going to leap forward and throw a bucket of green paint over the Queen? The day went by with boringly predictable smoothness; the parade was executed with precision as it was year after year; HM was her usual faultless self.

Fuming, Prior went home, irritated his wife, drank too much whisky, slept badly, woke on Sunday morning with a hangover and lay in till eleven o'clock and so missed all the fun of Londoners laughing at the capital's familiar statues, each one – except for those, like Nelson, the Duke of York and Prince Albert, inaccessible through height – crowned with a laurel wreath, like the ones awarded to medal-winners at the 2004 Olympic Games in Athens. Another colour of the spectrum had appeared. The day of green had arrived.

Before the American Embassy in Grosvenor Square both Franklin Delano Roosevelt on his lofty plinth and General Dwight Eisenhower in battledress had been honoured with a headdress of shiny green leaves. In the case of King George III in his ridiculous Roman apparel, standing in the imposing plaza of Somerset House off the Strand, surrounded by a lion and bits of symbolic naval paraphernalia, a laurel wreath did not seem so out of place.

Oliver Cromwell in front of the House of Commons, the Burghers of Calais in Victoria Tower Gardens and Rabbie Burns on the Embankment had all received their verdant crowns. There was no distinction of nationality or occupation. In Parliament Square Abraham Lincoln and

South African General Smuts, besides British Prime Ministers Lord Derby, Palmerston, Peel, Disraeli and of course Sir Winston Churchill, had all alike been honoured. John Wesley ('The world is my parish') outside his chapel in the City Road, Dr Johnson in the Strand, Queen Anne at St Paul's Cathedral; Edith Cavell in Charing Cross Road ('Patriotism is not enough'), Byron at Hyde Park Corner, Shakespeare in Leicester Square, Sir Joshua Reynolds in the forecourt of the Royal Academy in Piccadilly – wherever people strolled and chatted, wherever Sunday morning crowds gathered, throughout the area of central London previously decorated, every well-known public statue was favoured with a laurel crown. The accolade extended to the non-human and the semi-human – Peter Pan in Kensington Gardens, Eros in Piccadilly Circus, and the South Bank Lion at the end of Westminster Bridge.

And Downing Street? Received nothing. Security was on the alert all day, the secretaries in anticipation, but nothing came. Sniffer dogs were in readiness, bomb disposal experts on hand. Everybody who worked at no. 10 was on edge and the day's work was done with nervous irritability. They worked overtime and went home late, frustrated and exhausted. But contrary to appearances the PM had not been forgotten.

When dawn broke the following morning, the duty policeman in Parliament Square was startled to find a life-size figure tied to the railings outside Old Palace Yard, fronting the House of Commons. It was an artistically-made dummy, clearly recognisable as the Prime Minister. And he too had received his accolade; the head of the grotesque figure was crowned with a magnificent wreath of green laurel.

Prior leaped into action as soon as he heard this news. At last here was something he could get his teeth into. He immediately ordered the effigy to be removed and brought in for examination, but he was rather too late. The press had got there before his men arrived and a score of photographers ensured that the ridiculous figure, complete with verdant laurel wreath, appeared on all the front pages of the evening papers.

Surely this would give forensics more to go on, Prior reasoned. He ordered an exhaustive examination of the dummy and analysis of its materials, not ignoring the possibility of its containing a bomb. Green was the colour of the month, and green suggested Ireland. Sinn Fein? The IRA? Some new dissident Republican group?

No bomb was found, nor was any substantial evidence of any kind. The figure contained nothing but straw, paper, cloth and a bit of paint. Would the wreath tell them anything? It had been freshly cut. For a fleeting moment Prior thought of a police hunt throughout the capital to find laurel bushes or hedges that had been recently cut. How many would there be? Millions. And they might not have come from London anyway. The idea died a natural death.

He called for Hicks. If he was so bloody clever, let him solve this one.

'What do you make of it, Hicks? You've got another colour of the rainbow. How does that help us?'

'I can't say it does, Chief. Of course, I thought at first of the Green Party...' (Dammit, thought Prior, the Green Party – why didn't I think of that?) '... but there doesn't seen to be any point, because of all the other colours.'

'Well of course, it can't be the Green Party, that was obvious from the start,' Prior lied.

'Exactly, sir. There's only one other point I've noticed, but I don't suppose it's significant. I mean the lion theme.'

'Lion? We haven't had any bloody lions. What'd'ya mean?'

'Well, it's only a small thing, but it does connect the five incidents we've had so far. It's one thing they all have in common. We started with yellow, right? There were yellow wreaths round the lions in Trafalgar Square, like what they give you in Hawaii and places like that – Leis, I think they're called...'

'Yes. Well?'

'Then we had the purple water. It came out of various outlets, but at least one place reported was a fountain where the water came out of a lion's mouth.'

'Pure coincidence. The water was in all sorts of other places.'

'Yes, sir. It may not mean anything... But then came the oranges. They were left in a number of locations, but only one of them was addressed to an individual, if you remember, sir...'

'Of course I remember, Hicks. I've been on this damned case from the beginning.'

Prior searched his memory for the name.

'Lyon King-of-arms, one of the chief heralds at the College of Arms. The chief herald of Scotland,' Hicks prompted his superior.

'Bloody silly name.'

'Yes, sir. Traditional. Well, there's another lion.'

'Spelt L-Y-O-N, Hicks.'

'I know sir, but still a lion. That was the oranges. Next we had the red letters. They were only delivered to four streets, all with red in the name, and one of them—'

'Red Lion Square. Yes, it's certainly odd, though I'd still say coincidental.'

'And finally, the green laurel wreaths. One of them was placed on the head of the South Bank Lion.'

'Very impressive, Hicks. Any conclusions?'

'No, Chief, only facts. May or may not be significant. And there's one more thing. The Red Lion is at the south end of Westminster Bridge, the South Bank. The old Festival of Britain site.'

'I know that.'

'It's the only location south of the river in the whole series, that's all. It may or may not be—'

'Thank you, Hicks. Major terrorist attack on the Festival Hall within the next twenty-four hours, do you think?'

'No sir, I was only thinking—'

'Good, Hicks, you do just that. Go on thinking. And while you're doing that, just get on with some police work, if you don't want to find yourself down at the Job Centre.'

'Yes, sir. Thank you, sir.'

'Too clever by half,' muttered Prior as the door closed.

For the rest of the day lions circled in the Detective Chief Inspector's head. Another of Hick's daft ideas. Could there be anything in it? Lions in the zoo at Regent's Park; the British Lions – the Rugby team; the royal arms; the lion and the unicorn; Richard the Lion Heart; distant memories of Lyon's Corner House; Red Lion Square; Lyon King of fussing Arms; lions in books – Aslan, the lion in Narnia; *The Lion King*, the Disney musical, currently playing at the Lyceum Theatre in the Strand; Red Lion pubs all over the place... It was all irrelevant, all bloody – he grimaced at the irony of the word – nonsense. Nevertheless lions in their majesty rampaged through his dreams all night.

When Malcolm met Cordelia that evening in their favourite pub he crowned her with a delicately-made green laurel wreath, like an Olympic gold medal winner, in full view of everybody.

'My gold medal winner,' he said as he embraced her.

She was not displeased. The whole pub exploded in laughter and applause.

CHAPTER 14

That was the middle of June. For four months the story had run and run in the press, enhanced by theories and speculation about the meaning and motive of it all. The suspicion that the colours of the rainbow were somehow relevant and the fact that the attacks were roughly monthly had established themselves in the public mind. It was therefore pretty widely agreed that July would see another outburst of colour in London, and that the colour would almost certainly be blue. Sweepstakes were run on the probable date of the next incident; phone-in programmes on radio and television invited people's views; chat show hosts interrogated their guests on their favourite colour; the weekly magazines enjoyed the bonanza. There was a heady atmosphere in the town that London had not experienced since the Swinging Sixties and the glory days of Carnaby Street.

The thing that puzzled Prior and his colleagues most of all was that no CCTV cameras could supply them with any hard evidence. Either the incidents happened out of sight of a camera or the cameras had been temporarily masked. All they could gather from that was that the whole series of events must have been planned with military efficiency. The trouble was that the rate of normal street crime showed no signs of abating, so that police vigilance could not be relaxed in areas where real trouble was likely and the Met could hardly call in extra help from other Forces just to monitor an elaborate but harmless hoax that might not happen anyway. It was also clear to Prior that, since the Queen's Birthday had passed without incident, the gang appeared not to be interested in disrupting public events. Royal Ascot and the Garter Ceremony at Windsor, high profile events in the summer social calendar, had also gone off without a hitch. This made planning any sort of precautions for the next incident almost impossible. July offered no focal point that would attract more than usual publicity; the next display of colour could happen any time.

All Prior had was a hunch. Being only a hunch, he did not like to tell anyone – Hicks least of all – but his hunch centred on Trafalgar Square. The crazy gang had to be a large and coordinated group, and Prior believed that they must have a point to make. The chain of colour must be a lead-up to something. He envisaged some kind of rally or demonstration, and the most likely place was Trafalgar Square. Perhaps it was the lions prowling around his thoughts that subconsciously led him there.

His hunch would not let him rest. One day at the beginning of July he rose from his desk on an impulse and took his cap.

'I'm going out.'

'Yes, sir. Shall I call a car, sir?'

'No, I'll walk.'

Walking was better. He might get some insight along the way.

He cut through side streets into St James's Park and proceeded up Horse Guards' Road, noting significant buildings, statues, fountains. He passed the end of Downing Street. Surely he could crack this one. The chain of events was still running, perhaps heading for a climax. He must nail it now. He dreamed of the public recognition that success would bring. Perhaps even – he allowed himself the secret thought – a knighthood. Sir Norman Prior; it sounded good.

He emerged into The Mall and turned right under Admiralty Arch, pondering all the while, putting himself in the place of a gang of hooligans who were going to splash blue about somewhere and then hold a rally in Trafalgar Square.

The Square seemed quite normal, full of sightseers and pigeons, except that the area round Nelson's Column was screened off with scaffolding and hoarding, a sign on each side said CLEANING AND ROUTINE MAINTENANCE IN PROGRESS. Works' vehicles stood nearby and workmen went in and out of the hoarding. This reduced the area a little, but there was still space enough for a major rally.

Prior walked round, paying particular attention to the statues and the fountains, thinking, thinking, thinking. St Martin-in-the-Fields Church offered its usual mix of dossing for the homeless, brass-rubbing and lunchtime concerts. A Renaissance Exhibition was on at the National Gallery. He examined the cross at Charing Cross and stared hard at the frontages of South Africa House, Canada House, Uganda House... Everything was depressingly normal.

He questioned the police on the beat and gleaned nothing; he talked casually to street sweepers, the down-and-outs on the steps of St Martin's, the janitor at the National Gallery, a man on a newspaper stall; no one had anything odd to report.

Prior went over to the base of Nelson's Column and penetrated the screened area. Nothing but routine cleaning and maintenance seemed to be going on. Five or six men in overalls, dirty boots and yellow hard hats were working at the standard leisurely pace of manual workers. Another was drinking tea. Prior identified the foreman, in a collar and tie, holding a clipboard, and showed his ID.

'When did this job start?'

The foreman gave him details. He seemed polite and efficient.

'What's the job spec?'

The foreman showed him a sheaf of papers, which included diagrams.

'Routine cleaning, mostly. The side panels of the plinth are bronze. We use a particular chemical formula. I can give you details if you like.' He thumbed through the papers on his clipboard.

'That's all right. Certainly makes a difference.' Prior admired part of one of the huge bas-relief panels, depicting a scene from the 1805 Battle of Trafalgar, which had been cleaned. The bronze shone, in sharp contrast to the rest of the panel, which was dulled with decades of London grime.

'It takes quite a time,' the foreman went on. 'When we've finished the panels, then of course there're the lions. And then the stonework – that's not so simple. There's quite a lot of damage to the fabric, as you can see. Wearing on the corners, cracks and chips. Look at this one. That'll mean repair, probably a patch – a bit of new stone. Of course we have to get an exact match of the stone colour.'

'Yes, quite a job.' Prior was friendly. 'Do you get any trouble from the public? I mean, sightseers must be a bit frustrated, not being able to see the plinth and the lions.'

'People are very understanding on the whole. Yes, the tourists are disappointed, of course. They always want to take photographs of the lions. I thought myself, why do this job in the middle of the tourist season? But you can't argue with the boffins in the Borough Office. Anyway, we haven't had any trouble so far.'

'How long will it take?'

'End of the month. We hope to finish before the start of the school holidays if we can, but we may not make it by then.'

Prior took his leave. 'Thanks. I hope you do. And please let the police know if you have any trouble, or if you notice anything unusual going on in the Square.' He left his name and phone number.

He walked away and then stared hard at each access to the Square in turn and noted the flow of traffic: The Mall,

Cockspur Street, Charing Cross Road, the Strand, Northumberland Avenue, Whitehall. No ray of light dawned on his fuddled senses. He stopped in a pub to console himself for a wasted morning. He scowled suspiciously at everyone as if they were all foreign agents, illegal immigrants, criminals, vandals or suicide bombers, then finished his beer and walked back down Whitehall.

Malcolm finished his beer and got up to go back to work for the afternoon. Cordelia picked up her handbag. They had been finalising plans for the wedding. Not long to go now. It was certainly going to be different. For one thing, it was to be in the open air. Of course, Cordelia's parents didn't like it but it meant that there would be plenty of room. The guest list had grown and grown. They went over the words they would say… and the music. There would be a live band: seats for the band; everyone else was to be standing. Food and drink, trestle tables, the going-away, which was somewhat elaborate. The whole affair was to be a mixture of the simple and the intricate and certainly needed careful planning. Every detail was discussed, down to the carpet they were to stand on. Cordelia had insisted on a carpet.

CHAPTER 15

Most men regard weddings as a bit of a bore: hardly more than a chance to get mildly drunk at someone else's expense. And many men regard their own wedding in the same light; the symbolism means little. The fuss and bother, the negotiation with parents, the details of dress, the flowers, the photographs, the presents, the paraphernalia of ritual words and music, the meal, the reception, the dance, the going away – these things do not grip them. They look on them as things belonging to the feminine world, things that hardly concern them more than make-up and sanitary towels. They patiently endure the months of planning and preparation, slightly mystified by the importance these things have in the mind of their beloved.

Malcolm Romney was somewhat different. He was – the political term seemed not inappropriate – a radical. He was a thinker. He questioned the meaning and purpose of inherited mores, and if he found no good reason for perpetuating accepted norms of behaviour, he dropped them. But where he differed from the mass of anarchists, rebels and drop-outs of society was in his extraordinary gentleness. Nothing could be less like the usual anti-establishment activist. He was not a troublemaker and he sought no publicity. He simply had values, standards, ideas that sometimes ran counter to conventional patterns of society, and he expressed them quietly but firmly. He made people think.

As he approached his own wedding, Malcom did not discard the traditions that everybody expected with any sense of iconoclasm. He was neither a new-ager who wanted to be married in a beauty spot with propitious ley lines, nor an eccentric who chose a wedding in a hot-air balloon or under water. He simply thought through every aspect of the traditional wedding day and questioned whether it was meaningful or not.

What was more remarkable was that Cordelia thought the same way. It was partly this that had drawn them together. Their close agreement on every detail of the wedding day was indeed a marriage of true minds. A wedding that was right for them, that would say something to everyone present and even begin to change and challenge people's unthinking attitudes – that was their hope and their intention. They wanted to do things differently, not for the sake of difference but for the sake of meaning.

'Therefore shall a man leave his father and mother, and cleave to his wife.' The ancient words of the wedding liturgy, words from the oldest part of the Bible itself, ringing down through four millennia, were their guide. They both enjoyed good relations with their parents, and yet here was ancient precedent for acting independently and they brought the principle into effect not from the moment of marriage but from the moment of engagement. Consequently, both their parents were firmly excluded from the wedding plans. Malcolm and Cordelia were both in good jobs and had saved judicially; they were not dependent on their parents for the expenses of the wedding. These were, in any case, going to be much more modest than the average of some £10,000 spent on weddings in Britain.

And so it came about that Malcolm really enjoyed the preparations for his wedding. He and Cordelia agreed on almost every point and shared their plans with a small circle of friends, which included the Rev. Antony Kilbride. The operation went smoothly, without the inter-family friction that so often plagues weddings as the day approaches. And although they were not involving their own families in the planning, they kept them fully informed. There was a sunny openness about their way of doing things that conciliated others and avoided unseemly clashes. Every couple wants their day to be the acme of happiness, but this is so often spoiled by the tensions and conflicts of the weeks before.

Malcolm was a born planner. As July wore on, he was increasingly busy with things besides the wedding, and after-work meetings with a group of friends occupied many evenings. A sense of growing excitement inspired them, a sense of climax like that of any period leading up to a wedding, but which would extend beyond the wedding day itself, into a future whose outcome no one could certainly foresee.

CHAPTER 16

It was late on the afternoon of Friday, 22 July that an enormous basket of top quality delphiniums was delivered to Buckingham Palace, addressed to the Queen herself. The parcel was well wrapped in blue paper, and a prominent Royal Arms was displayed on the lid – blazing colours, red, blue and gold, lions and harp, *Honi Soit Qui Mal Y Pense*: the lot. As before, the press had been tipped off by an anonymous phone call, but the difference was that the time was announced beforehand, so that cameramen were there when the delivery was made. It came in a small unmarked van. They mobbed the driver, a woman, for information, but she either knew nothing of the origin of the flowers or was not talking. When Prior got news of the event he was furious with security for letting the van go.

The result was that, unlike the previous incidents, this one made it big on the front pages of the morning papers the following day, Saturday, as well as the TV and radio news. No one doubted that the innocent gesture was the culmination of the colour series, the completion of the rainbow. Everyone felt it was appropriate that the recipient of the flowers was not the Prime Minister this time but the Queen. It was obviously intended as a climax. The day of blue had arrived.

Right again! thought Hicks as he devoured the papers, enjoying the pleasure of the hunt without the responsibility. Blue. I knew it would be. And lions again!, as he noted a picture of the royal arms on the box. I knew it. In fact, seven of them. Six yellow and one red. There must be a meaning in it...

A climax? More like a frigging anti-climax, mused Prior.

A bunch of flustering flowers! He went through the wearisome routine of sending men to question the security staff at the Palace and the servant who had received the bouquet, and make a thorough examination of the flowers, though he was not, of course, expecting anything. At the same time he could not believe that this was all. Once again he rang his colleagues at the Met and asked for extra vigilance in central London. Anything out of the ordinary was to be reported to him immediately; especially, of course, they were to look out for any signs of blue. He had a fast car on standby.

Amanda was drunk with excitement. Harry had received the tip-off in good time on the Friday afternoon and she was his chosen apostle. Accompanied by Marcus and his equipment as usual, she was on the scene ahead of rival reporters. The delivery van drove up to the side gate of Buckingham Palace at 5.15 p.m. It was not allowed inside, so the flowers were handed over at the gate, giving Marcus plenty of opportunity for shots at various angles. He also photographed the van, though it had no name or identifying marks anywhere, and the driver, a woman. Amanda questioned her. Even with her professional techniques, her knowing charm, her dogged persistence, she got nothing. The driver was taciturn, acted as if she was an idiot or a deaf mute. There was absolutely no response to any of Amanda's questions.

'Could you tell us where the flowers come from?'
'Why are flowers being given to the Queen today?'
'Are you the registered owner of this van?'
'Who ordered the flowers?'
'Surely you must have a delivery note?'
'Do you know why delphiniums have been chosen?'
'Did you personally place any of the laurel wreaths?'
'Have you delivered things to Buckingham Palace before?'

And then, exasperated: 'We'll make it worth your while. If you could come along to our office and give us the whole story, I think you'll find my paper will be very generous. It could even be a five-figure sum...'

It was some time before Amanda realised that the driver was literally deaf and dumb and gave up the barrage of questions. The clever bastards. They wanted the publicity but were covering their tracks as well. She tried scribbling down this tempting promise on her notepad to show the girl but before she could finish the driver had swung herself into the cab and driven off down Buckingham Gate, and was lost in the traffic. All Amanda could do was note the registration number of the van. She then phoned the police and told them the number, hoping perhaps for some recognition. Amanda's mind ran on headlines, and she pictured this one: 'Newspaper woman's prompt action leads to arrest', 'Mystery flowers traced through reporter's canniness', 'Woman journalist leads to colour hoax discovery'. She took care to give the police her name and phone number.

She sent in her story and remained on the streets in central London, waiting for further calls from Harry. Like everyone else, she recognised the event as the next, probably the last, in the chain of colour incidents: another colour of the rainbow. She had no doubt that other blue phenomena would appear somewhere in London and kept in close contact with Harry for any further sightings. She hung around until the blue faded out of the sky; darkness in this midsummer season did not come till 10 p.m. Dog-tired, she caught the Tube home and went straight to bed, phone by bedside, ready for an early start in the morning or perhaps another call in the early hours.

Saturday 23 July. Amanda was up early. She showered and prepared for the day. She checked into the office before eight, and read her own frustratingly limited account of the incident of the flowers in the morning edition. She then experienced the occupational hazard of a long wait. The office buzzed around her but nothing in her particular field came in for two hours. It seemed a long time between coffees. Finally, shortly before 10 a.m. the first hint of something happening came in. Harry took the call; Amanda and others crowded round.

CHAPTER 17

Four large lorries had arrived in Trafalgar Square and parked close to Nelson's Column, up against the scaffolding around the plinth. Being a Saturday, there was no work going on. Instead of the usual workmen, a motley group of people had started emerging from all four trucks. This was the spur for action. With a nod from Harry, Amanda was soon speeding on her way.

As soon as the duty officer in the Square saw what was happening he rang Prior on his direct line, as he had been instructed. Prior chortled inwardly when he heard the news. Trafalgar Square – I knew it, I bloody knew it! He barked his orders.

'I'm on my way. Keep watching them. Note anything unusual. Call some more men to the scene. Get the numbers of those lorries. And don't let any of them drive away. I'll be with you in five minutes.'

He was. He arrived melodramatically on the scene with siren blaring. Other Scotland Yard men followed. A dozen officers of the Metropolitan Police had assembled. They reported to Prior for instructions.

'Just hold back and await orders. I want you deployed around the Square. Report any suspicious movements. Keep in touch. Wait for my next order, and watch them like bloody lynxes.'

Hicks was at his side. The irrepressible Hicks.

'Shall I question them, sir? Shall I get those lorries moved?'

'No, no need to yet. We'll just wait and see what they get up to. May be harmless…'

It certainly seemed harmless. Dozens of people had

appeared from the lorries and fanned out into the Square. There must have been more than a hundred. They were all casually dressed; jeans, tee shirts and trainers were the norm – but the dress was noticeably colourful, so that the Square took on the appearance of a fiesta. Some carried folding chairs and set them up; others had music stands and sound equipment, mikes, amps, speakers, yards of cable. Musicians took their seats and started tuning up.

'A gig,' murmured Hicks. 'The ruddy cheek!'

The morning crowds, commuters, shoppers, sightseers, began to gather around the sides of the Square. Those not in a hurry hung about, idly watching the preparations as more and more stuff emerged from the lorries. Some of the people carried bins and brushes and went around the area systematically sweeping and picking up litter.

Suddenly there was an audible gasp from the crowd, a movement of concentration from the police and even a stir of excitement from passing traffic. People in cars and buses stared and a buzz ran around the Square. From the lorries more people alighted carrying vases and pedestals of ready-made flower arrangements, which they placed around the central plaza. There were agapanthus, hyacinths, larkspurs, delphiniums, and hydrangeas. All the flowers were blue.

The statues around the Square were appropriately decorated with flowers – that random selection of long-forgotten heroes of the age of empire: Havelock, Napier, Beatty, Jellicoe, Cunningham – to which the public were now totally indifferent, together with the more historic equestrian sculpture of King Charles I, 'the fair and fatal king,' not far from the place of his execution that had sparked the Civil War in 1649. Flowers were everywhere. The atmosphere of festivity was palpable.

The tide of chatter and laughter rose. Crowds attracted crowds. The police looked at each other, closed in a step or two, looked towards Prior. He made no movement but gasped and stared in disbelief as more people backed out of one of the lorries carrying, with some difficulty, several huge rolls of blue carpet, which they proceeded to spread out on the plaza, covering a considerable area. They moved quietly and efficiently, happily talking and laughing in the most innocent manner. There was no shouting, no rowdiness, no indecent behaviour. The clock on the church tower of St Martin in the Fields struck eleven.

'Shall I book them, Chief?'

'It's not a crime, Hicks.' Still he made no move, but he was thinking furiously. Blue Day had arrived. Assuming they could forget the drab and elusive colour called indigo, the rainbow was complete. He had no doubt that it was the same gang – the crazy gang. They knew exactly what they were doing and the whole thing must have been planned to the letter. But the inconsistency of the chain of events tormented him. Five times the gang had worked in a single night, undercover, remaining completely anonymous; five times Downing Street had received a missive of some kind. Now, Buckingham Palace was the beneficiary, and here was the eruption of colour happening not at night but in the most public way possible in broad daylight on a sunny July morning.

In spite of his frustrations, Prior inwardly began to relax and even to enjoy the bizarre spectacle, while watching every movement alertly. The whole charade could be a blind for something far more sinister. He imagined the wrath of his superiors and his public disgrace if he allowed a terrorist attack to take place under his nose. He was also well aware that the whole thing might be a well-planned diversion while a crime was taking place elsewhere, and he warned the police network accordingly.

The band now started playing a medley of easy-listening music, well within reasonable limits, much to the delight of the gathering crowd. A ripple of laughter went up as they recognised the *Blue Danube Waltz*; a selection of blues and jazz followed. Trestle-tables were set up, food and drink laid out. A cake appeared. Meanwhile some of the people in the centre walked around the crowd, handing out small bunches of blue flowers. They were cheerful and friendly, but to queries of 'What's going on?' responded only, 'You'll see.' Blue balloons, little blue flags and blue paper streamers were distributed to the children. One almost expected the presenters of Blue Peter to appear. Trafalgar Square radiated blueness.

'We'll get them under the Anti-Litter Act, if nothing else' Hicks growled to himself.

The crowds thickened; more police were called in, silent, waiting, good-humoured; the lorries remained; the music continued. Anticipation grew. The blue-carpeted area in front of the band remained empty. It seemed it was not just a concert. Everyone instinctively felt that at twelve o'clock something would happen, and all except the urgently busy lingered to see what it would be. A few minutes before noon the band started on a competent rendering of Gershwin's *Rhapsody in Blue*. London swung to the schmaltzy rhythm. And coming up from the river, some kind of procession appeared along Northumberland Avenue. The crowd swayed back and with a surge of anticipation all heads were turned in that direction.

'Look, they're coming!'

'Who are?'

'There's masses of them. Look! Laughing and singing!'

'Who on earth are they?'

'What's it all about? Must be a demo of some kind.'

'They're on a wagon.'

'A what?'

'A wagon, a farm wagon. With a horse. Look!'

Excitement ran through the crowd, the noise escalated, almost drowning the music, as the improbable party of happy, colourful people, cheering and laughing, reached the end of Northumberland Avenue and emerged into the Square.

CHAPTER 18

No one could believe at first that it was going to be a genuine wedding. True, the laws on marriage had relaxed and marriages were being held all over the place, but in the middle of a crowded square, surrounded by strangers, seemed an unlikely venue. In fact everything about it was unlikely; but a wedding it was. The bridal party arrived in a farm wagon drawn by a horse and decorated with blue ribbons, crowded with talking, laughing, singing, waving, jostling friends. The bride was unmistakable, in a very simple white dress with a small bouquet of blue flowers, but everyone else was in the same casual but colourful attire as the people who had arrived by lorry. The wagon reached the Square, to tumultuous laughter and cheers, and everyone got out. With hilarity, but no rowdiness, they made their way to the blue carpet, swaying to the rhythm of the music, where the bride and groom took their places without ceremony in front of a tall young man who seemed to act with some authority, although he did not look like a minister or registrar.

By this time the press were on the scene in force. There was much scribbling on notepads, chattering on mobile phones, flashing of cameras, rolling of video film.

Amanda and Marcus were there with the rest.

Despite the excitement, Amanda was weary. She felt she deserved better. She felt the whole story – the patient months of waiting, the long unsocial hours, the constant being on the alert for every outbreak of colour in London – was her particular scoop. It was hard to share it. But a score or more of pushy newspaper men jostled around her. Journalism was a competitive business and here was the competition in force. It was humiliating to be just one of a crowd when she had led the field from the beginning. Nevertheless, dedicated professional that she was, she concentrated on the job. This was certainly a climax, and she was not going to fail at the last hurdle.

Where do we go from here? mused Hicks. Prior was racking his brains to remember the current state of marriage law. He dispatched an officer to a police van where there was a laptop, to look it up on the Internet. Did the location have to be a registered venue? What was the law on registration?

When he turned back to the scene of action, things had begun to happen. The clock of St Martin's in the Fields, fronting the Square, chimed twelve. The band finished the Gershwin and after a short pause struck up a modern song, in which the whole assembly spontaneously joined. There were no song books, no projector or screen, but they obviously knew the song well. The crowd noise died. Prior listened, fascinated. The song had a strange, unearthly beauty. Now strong and confident, now gentle and wistful, it rang through the Square. The style was contemporary but it had a hymn-like resonance. An acre of peace was created amid the turbulence of a London Saturday. The traffic slowed. Against all the odds, a touch of the holy manifested itself. What was going on could only be called worship.

Prior decided to act. He was well aware that no offence had been committed so far; he would simply question the whole proceeding. He would keep it low-key: a quiet word with the man in charge. As soon as the song was finished, he moved forward as unobtrusively as possible and approached the tall young man.

'I'd like a word, if I may.'

'Yes, Inspector?'

'No need to be alarmed. Nice ceremony you've got going here. What's it all about? Just checking.'

'It's a wedding.'

'Right. Very nice, too. We just have to make sure that everything is in order. Do you have authority to conduct weddings?'

'Yes. I am a minister of religion.' Prior stared at the man's informal dress, but could not think of anything sensible to say. The man simply waited. Then, 'This is my licence to officiate, if you want it.' He produced a paper from his pocket.

Prior read 'Diocese of London. To our well-beloved in Christ Antony James Kilbride, of... etc. etc., I hereby grant you permission until...31 December... to exercise the office of... hm hm... Signed, James Londin +. I see. Thank you.' He handed the paper back. Londin plus: what sort of a name was that? He was not familiar with ecclesiastical Latin or the strange conventions of the national church.

'So you intend to register the marriage here?' Prior was still playing for time, waiting to hear from his subordinate whether a wedding in Trafalgar Square was legal. He need not have bothered.

'No. This couple are married already.'

'But you say this is a wedding?'

'A wedding, part two, you could call it. The important part. The couple were legally married this morning.'

'And what is the important part?'

'Marriage before God.'

This was a poser. Prior's mouth was half open to express some clinching sarcasm, but as nothing occurred to him, he shut it again. He wisely decided to play it cool.

'Ah. A religious ceremony. You belong to a religious sect?'

The man paused, considering the word sect. 'Well, that's a loaded word. I would prefer the word section; one section of the universal church. It's called the Church of England.'

'My God!' The expression escaped from Prior's lips

involuntarily. Before he had time to think, the young man returned, quietly, with the hint of a smile, 'I'm glad to hear that you too are a believer.'

Prior felt wrong-footed and annoyed with himself, but pursued his questions. 'This young couple are married already? Then they have a certificate?'

'Actually, I have it, Inspector. Here it is.' Again he drew a folded paper from his pocket.

I'm making an ass of myself, thought Prior, not for the first time. 'Thank you.' He scrutinised the document. He read: 'Marriage solemnized at the Lambeth Registry Office, London, 23 July 20—, between Malcolm Luke Romney, bachelor, civil engineer, of... yes, yes... and Cordelia Bridget Beckford, spinster, interior decorator, of... hm, hm... according to the Provisions of the Marriage Act... signed... in the presence of us... yes... I, Nathaniel Rolfe, registrar, do hereby certify that this is a true copy of... hm, hm... Good. That seems to be in order. But why not in a church, may I ask?'

'We have nothing against churches,' said Antony. 'In fact, I think you'll find that everybody here is a committed member of a local church. Malcolm and Cordelia preferred to hold this service in the open air, that's all.'

'The open air. Of course, that's fine. But why not in the countryside, or in a garden? Why choose the most public place in London?'

'Because it's a witness. A marriage is a witness to Christian values. Our master said, "Let your light shine before men, that they may see your good deeds and praise your Father in heaven."'

So they're just religious nutters, Prior said to himself. As I thought: the whole freaking business is totally harmless. And he boiled inwardly to think how much valuable police time had been wasted by this pathetic pantomime. He felt sick of the whole business. All he could do was humour them.

'Right, splendid, splendid. Well, I'll leave you to your shining, then.' He even managed a watery smile, a handshake with Antony and a brusque congratulatory address to the happy pair, before turning away to consider his next move. He sighed heavily, aware that the cordon of police around the Square were all looking in his direction. At last he made his decision and spoke quietly into his radio mike. He reduced the police presence on the site by half. Some of the police vehicles moved away discreetly. He ordered continued vigilance from the rest.

'Keep well back, but keep watching. We'll stay till this crapulous comic opera is over. It's all lovey-dovey at the moment: just make sure it stays that way. And watch out for any nastiness. These wimps are probably extremists. Fundamentalists. Look out for anti-Semitism or anything anti-Muslim – that's more likely. Anything that smacks of religious hatred. They're probably far right... Anything like that, we'll drop on them.'

The service proceeded. Antony managed to combine a sense of dignity with a spontaneous kind of joy, which infected the mood of the whole congregation. There was a framework of time-honoured words, including the vows, interspersed with informal readings, greetings and prayers. The music was neither predictably traditional nor brashly modernist; it was original, yet caught everyone up in an aura of praise. The whole Square was hushed and attentive and the crowds seemed to be entering into the joyous solemnity of the occasion. Malcolm and Cordelia were radiant and their happiness communicated itself to the ranks of onlookers. Everyone was entranced by Cordelia with her flaming red hair.

There seemed to be no break between religious service and reception. After more singing, the proceedings moved smoothly into tributes, expressions of affection, thanks, good wishes, from all and sundry, including little poems and spontaneous songs, a far cry from the laboriously composed formal speeches of father, best man and groom, with their predictable banter at the traditional wedding. Drinks were handed round and trays of finger food; toasts were drunk; the cake was cut. Dancing followed, the blue carpet becoming a dance floor. The crowds around seemed to get caught up in the mood until the whole Square was a swaying, dancing, laughing mass. The only people not totally happy were four smartly-dressed, middle-aged, middle-class onlookers who clubbed together on the fringe of the party; Mr and Mrs Romney; Mr and Mrs Beckford.

Reporters at the front of the crowd were scribbling, phoning, flashing, gleefully composing headlines for the morning papers:

RHAPSODY IN BLUE;

SOMETHING BORROWED, SOMETHING BLUE;

LOVE ME TENDER, LOVE ME BLUE;

BLUE RIBAND FOR THE BRIDE;

RECIPE FOR MARRIED BLISS – CORDON BLEU;

WEDDING PAIR LAY DOWN THE BLUE CARPET.

Amanda and Marcus did their best.

The ceremony came to a climax in the traditional wedding march, a midsummer night's dream of melody. The band excelled itself; Oberon and Titania danced unseen among the crowd; Shakespeare and Mendlessohn walked tiptoe across the plaza; and the congregation, led by the bride and groom, turned towards the east side of the Square. The crowds parted to let them through and the police kept a watchful eye as the whole party moved slowly in the direction of Charing Cross Station amid laughing and cheering. At the same time, without warning and without waiting to pick up any of the equipment, the four huge lorries moved quietly away, dispersing in different directions: one northwards up Charing Cross Road, one to the west along Cockspur Street, one turning south down Whitehall and the other making for the river along Northumberland Avenue. Prior noticed this with indefinable misgivings. The wedding was over, but the party was just beginning.

CHAPTER 19

Prior later remembered this as the worst, and yet the best, moment of the whole case. It was the worst because after a frustrating and time-wasting day, when he was beginning to think the series of demonstrations was at an end and he could forget the whole pathetic business, something serious occurred, leaving him baffled once again; but the best because now he had something to get his teeth into. At last, here was something that had the unmistakeable aspect of a crime.

Hicks had noticed it at the same time and was at his superior's side. Turning back after the wedding procession had left the Square on the east side, drawing all the attention of the crowds that way, he saw that the scaffolding along the west side of the plinth of Nelson's Column had been removed, along with the hoarding that screened it from public view. And at one corner of the plinth there was a gaping emptiness.

Everyone, Londoners and visitors alike, knew that at the four corners of the plinth were four gigantic bronze lions, sculpted by the popular Victorian artist Sir Edwin Landseer. They attracted much more attention than Nelson himself; his statue was in any case 170 feet up – far too high for anyone to see much. But the lions were the delight of tourists, who had to be photographed in front of them, and of adventurous children, who tried to climb on top of them. Now, the crowd stared in total unbelief at the place where a lion should have been. One of Sir Edwin's four monumental lions was missing.

For a short time Prior's mind went blank. Thoughts swirled so thickly in his brain that everything seemed to switch off. A kaleidoscope of ideas battered his consciousness – colours; national outrage, theft, vandalism, obstructing the police, lions, demonstration, blue flowers, riots, terrorism, political protest, religious extremism, blue carpets, weddings, lorries, Charing Cross – leaving him mentally paralysed. At last he got a grip on himself and focussed his mind. Once he started giving out orders, sanity returned.

'Hicks, follow the wedding party. They can't have got far. I want that man Kilbride, and the couple. What was the name? Romney. Bring them in, but play it cool, just for questioning. Johnson!'

'Sir?'

'I want those lorries followed. One of them must have the lion. The other three are a blind. We'll have to chase all four to get the right one. You've got the registration numbers. How many vehicles have we got here? Enough? Good. Report to me as soon as you catch them. Go, go, go!

'Mathers, you stay here. How many men have you got? Right. Seal off this area. Watch for anything else in the Square. We're dealing with some clever bastards here. Don't let's be fooled again.'

The peace of the Square was shattered. Crowds now swarmed around the plinth, gaping at where the lion should have been. The press pushed their way in, desperate to get reports in in time for the evening papers. Amanda was almost in a daze of happiness. It was a journalist's paradise, a reporter's dream. She had been up with the story from the start; she was on the spot now, and she was one of the first to contact her office.

Harry chortled and shouted to his staff while still on the phone to Amanda. 'Everyone on standby. Breaking news. Stop press. It gets better. Just the job. A lion! A bloody lion!' And to Amanda, 'Get pictures. Tell Marcus to get off his bum. Get them in quick. Yes, we're standing by. Lorries?... What, a wedding?... A wedding in Trafalgar Square?... This is fantastic! OK, text me your report right away. This is bloody marvellous. Give me all the detail you can. I want detail.' The office buzzed.

Prior remained in the Square, and very soon his phone was ringing. It was Hicks.

'We've got them, sir, Kilbride, and the couple. We're on the forecourt of Charing Cross Station. They were going for a train.'

'Well done. Have you got a car there? Right, bring them back to the Yard. I'll see you there.' He rang off. 'Mathers!'

'Sir?'

'How many men have you got? About twenty? Right, keep them here. Patrol the Square and report to me at intervals. Don't question anybody, unless there's a breach of public order. Just watch. Some of them'll be coming back to collect the equipment.'

Although the lorries had gone and the band with their instruments had dispersed with the rest of the wedding party, the blue carpet, chairs, flowers, tables and the amplifying system all remained. They were small beer compared to a bronze animal that weighed several tons and was a world-famous national icon. They were quietly collected in small vans and removed later in the day. Every scrap of litter was meticulously collected and the whole area swept clean by cheerful volunteers.

Prior took a quick walk around the whole site, fought off some reporters who were pressing for a statement, went back to his car and drove off, sounding his siren unnecessarily down Whitehall, Parliament Square and Victoria Street, to vent his feelings of mingled triumph and frustration. At last he had someone to interview, and that felt good. But it was a gamble. If Kilbride and the Romneys were as innocent as they looked, and had nothing to do with the lion's disappearance, he would be back to square one, he mused – and grunted at the irony of the unintended pun. But at least the press need not know *that* part of the story...

CHAPTER 20

The interviews at Scotland Yard were the most bizarre in Prior's experience; he kept the tape for years afterwards and sometimes played it for sheer entertainment value, even though he himself did not come out of it well. He could not repress a grudging admiration for his opponents. As Holmes recognised the talents of Moriarty, he acknowledged something unique in the bearing of his three detainees. He had interviewed polite, innocent-seeming, middle-class people scores of times; he had interviewed religious fanatics; he had interviewed professional criminals; he had interviewed suspects who remained perfectly calm and self-possessed under questioning. Here he seemed to be meeting those qualities all combined.

He questioned them one by one but could not find any discrepancy in the three stories. The attitude and responses of the three were the same and sounded as if they were well prepared. It became obvious that they had not only expected to be arrested, but wanted to be. They wanted publicity; they were concerned, as they put it themselves, to be witnesses, though their interpretation of the word was not that of the police. He questioned Kilbride.

'You are entitled to legal representation. Do you wish to call a lawyer?'

'No, thank you. Not at this stage.'

'You say you are witnesses. I presume you mean that in a religious sense? Are you Jehovah's Witnesses?'

'It depends how you write it.'

'What do you mean by that?'

'If "witness" has a capital letter, no. We believe they are a deviation from the truth. Jehovah is a Biblical name for God in some translations; we certainly aim to be his witnesses. I told you, we are members of the Church of England. Our churches can vouch for us.'

'You are aware that by holding a ceremony in the middle of Trafalgar Square you were causing considerable disruption, monopolising public space, causing danger to traffic, offending against the litter act and wasting an enormous amount of police time?'

'May I answer those charges one by one? One, I don't know what you mean by disruption; some people would call it entertainment, others would call it worship. Two, you say that the Square is public space; well, we are the public. Three, we were careful not to cause any obstruction to traffic and were concerned with safety throughout. Four, I don't think you will find any litter dropped by our people. In fact, some of them did some voluntary litter-picking during the day – other people's litter. Five, I believe the police presence was not necessary. The ceremony we held was in no way a threat to public order.'

Prior, wrong-footed, bluffed it out. The more frustrated he got, the more inflated and pompous became his language.

'We shall see. I can assure you a detailed investigation is going on. I think you may find that there is considerable evidence that a serious public nuisance has been caused. We'll come back to that. Now, you may or may not be aware that towards the close of your 'ceremony', as you call it, a very grave breach of public order was committed in the vicinity, an act of theft of considerable magnitude, a larceny of such—'

'You mean the lion?'

The duty sergeant standing behind Prior bit his lip to try to hide his involuntary smile. Prior scowled.

'Ah, so you know about the theft of the lion?'

'Yes, Inspector. We took it. But we don't regard it as theft.'

The sergeant almost whistled. Prior struggled to keep his cool.

'Who is "we"?'

'Members of our society. Friends who were present at the wedding.'

'Ah, now we're getting somewhere. So you belong to a secret society?'

'Not secret.'

'Well?'

'I told you before. We are all members of the Church of England.'

'Would you call the Church of England a society?'

'I don't see why not. A "company", if you prefer that word. That is what the Book of Common Prayer calls it: "The blessed company of all faithful men".'

'Are you members of the Prayer Book Society?'

'No. Just the Church of England.'

'We'll get back to the lion, if you don't mind,' said Prior with heavy sarcasm, disregarding the fact that he was the one who had caused the digression. 'You say that friends of yours, members of your wedding party, removed one of the lions from the base of Nelson's Column. Why?'

The answer moved the petty interview into the realm of theology, but a theology earthed in a passionate concern for people and a social awareness that could not be dismissed. The drab interview room became a council chamber, a high court, a conference hall. It took on the aura of a cathedral, a temple, a university, a parliament. The issues became national. The perspective expanded to the dimension of history.

All three of those questioned seemed as if they had been waiting for this opportunity. This was the focal point of all they stood for. But to handle the argument was not easy, and depended on Prior's willingness to take them seriously. It was a tall order to engage his attention on a serious level, and not have him dismiss them as mindless troublemakers.

'Why?' asked Prior. There was a pregnant pause.

'A lion is a symbol.'

'Go on.'

'A symbol of the nation, perhaps? Most people would see it like that. The British lion.'

Prior nodded involuntarily. He was 'most people'.

'We see it as much more than that, much more important, much more significant. A lion represents something eternal: the one who was, and is, and is to come.'

Prior rolled his eyes in exasperation. Here we go again, he thought, religious claptrap, and the expletive 'Christ!' muttered under his breath, escaped his lips. But it had been heard.

'Yes, Christ. That's who we mean.' The answer was still measured, patient, polite. 'You may remember Narnia?'

'Christ!' said Prior again, unthinkingly. 'Where are we going next? Middle Earth? Hogwarts' Hall? Can we stick to reality?'

'Reality is what we are concerned with. In the Narnia books, there is a lion. He is called Aslan. He is the voice of sanity and goodness and justice. He is killed, and rises again. He is Christ.'

'Are you telling me you're basing your crackpot philosophy on a children's book?'

'No, on the book of books: the Bible. It describes Christ as the Lion of the Tribe of Judah.'

'Are you Zionists? British Israelites?'

'No, we just believe that the Bible is relevant to our situation. We believe modern western society is sick, because it has turned away from God. It has forgotten the Bible. It has rejected Christ.'

'Spare me the sermon.'

'I'm sorry. It isn't meant to be a sermon, it's the explanation for what we have done.'

'Well then, explain.'

'We have removed a bronze lion, a symbol. We believe modern society has done a far more terrible thing: it has removed Christ, the Lion of Judah, from our national life. It has flouted Christian standards. We do not regard what we have done as theft. We have done no damage to the lion and we'll restore it in due time. I admit we did it for maximum publicity. We want the nation to hear our message.'

Prior tried a new tack.

'Theft it certainly is, and totally irresponsible. You are blissfully confident of your precious beliefs, but you may have noticed that in the twenty-first century we are a multicultural society. Talking of Christian standards is inappropriate in today's world. It's offensive to Jews and Muslims, for a start.'

I'm sorry, but I don't accept that. We have several Jewish and Muslim friends. They are sincere believers in their own creeds. We consulted them fully before taking action. They approve one hundred percent of what we are doing. They are with us all the way. They have not asked us to compromise our Christian convictions: in fact they have asked us not to.'

Prior's mind moved up a gear at the mention of Muslims. In the context of his work, and according to his ingrained prejudice, Muslim was almost synonymous with terrorist. Yet here was a so-called Christian claiming association with these troublemakers, and causing trouble themselves in the name of their belief. It didn't make sense.

'You have Muslim friends? I shall want their names and addresses later.'

'Certainly, I'm sure they won't object. They have nothing to hide. Neither have we. Perhaps you would like to investigate the church I serve?' Antony named it. 'I've been building bridges with Muslims for some years now. I see it as an important part of my ministry to the people who work in my parish.'

Prior seemed to be gaining no ground, and to be losing points at every turn. A knock at the door came to his rescue. The duty constable entered with a message, which he whispered in Prior's ear.

'First of the four lorries found, sir. B58 WDX. South London. Nothing in it.'

Prior used this as an excuse to end the interview.

'We'll await further evidence. I'm detaining you, and Mr and Mrs Romney, for further questioning. I'm charging you with causing an obstruction and wasting police time. You may apply for bail if you wish. But I warn you, I view this whole episode as extremely serious. Interview ends 3.25 p.m.' He switched off the tape.

'I'm glad we agree on that,' said Antony Kilbride, in the most respectful tone.

CHAPTER 21

Malcolm and Cordelia spent their wedding night in a police cell. They were not surprised; in fact, they had planned it that way. They had refused to apply for bail, in spite of the strenuous protests of their parents, who spent a wretched evening commiserating with each other. The papers loved it and the Sunday tabloids made a bonanza of it, pulling out all the stops in the headline department:

HOLY PADLOCK FOR NEWLY-WEDS;

ENGLAND EXPECTS THAT EVERY BRIDE WILL DO HER DUTY;

CELL-BY DATE FOR WEDDING COUPLE;

PASSION BEHIND BARS;

WEDLOCK OR DEADLOCK?;

BRIDEWELL FOR THE BRIDE.

The jailers in charge treated the whole thing with good humour; it was a pleasant break from their sordid routine. They allowed their charges to share a cell, slipped in some extra food and a bottle of wine, and had considerable sympathy for the couple. The male staff of course fell in love with Cordelia from the start and fought each other over who would take things to the cell.

But at last they were left in what passes for peace in a police lock-up. They were alone. They were tired but triumphant. Five months of planning and plotting had paid off. With their associates they had made a major impact on London and the media; the lion exploit, which nobody quite believed would come off, had gone like a dream.

Ahead of them stretched days, perhaps weeks, of questionings and court hearings. It was exactly what they wanted. They were ready for it. It was the opportunity they needed to argue a cause in which they passionately believed, and to do it with maximum publicity.

If stone walls do not a prison make, nor iron bars a cage, they proved it then. Minds innocent and quiet take that for a hermitage. Their minds were innocent and quiet.

They were not afraid.

Now they could relax. It was their wedding night. A little discomfort did nothing to mar their happiness. They were together. Very slowly, almost hesitantly, almost as if for the first time, they began to explore each other. Laughter came easily. They were drunk with excitement.

'What shall Cordelia speak?'

'Love, and be silent.'

They knew bits of King Lear by heart.

'I want you, I want all of you,' Malcolm whispered. 'You're so wonderful! I don't deserve this. I can't believe you said yes! You said yes to me! You actually said, "I will". Are you sure you haven't got the wrong man?'

'No contest,' she smiled. 'There's no one else, there's only you!'

Her kisses were gentle, shy, sensitive. Slowly, very slowly, they gave themselves to each other, hoping that no screw would choose to burst in on them. Malcolm found his love going deeper, deeper, admiring more and more her qualities of character and spirit as they drew together in one-flesh union, as if the meeting of bodies meant nothing without the meeting of minds and hearts. Cordelia found in his tenderness, his care for her, the consummation of the person she had come to love. And they both found that their passionate belief in a way of marriage so alien from the culture of the time, their dedication to chastity before marriage, was gloriously confirmed and vindicated by the joy of that night. Love was meant to be like this; they knew it beyond all doubt.

Angels alone that soar above enjoy such liberty.

Four unhappy people, Mr and Mrs Beckford, Mr and Mrs Romney, spent a sleepless night, dreading what they would find in the Sunday papers and on the breakfast news...

Prior went back to his office that Saturday afternoon, and heard the report of the lorry chase. The police had caught up with it in South London. Leaving Trafalgar Square it had run east down Northumberland Avenue to the river, turned south along the Victoria Embankment, over Westminster Bridge, then south through Kennington and Camberwell to Peckham. The police car had no difficulty in overtaking it, nor in stopping it. A glance inside the lorry revealed no thirty-foot lion. In fact it was totally empty. It was thoroughly searched and revealed nothing suspicious. The driver and an assistant were brightly dressed, cheerful and respectful. The police took their names and addresses. They asked the whereabouts of the lion, but the men were not talking. They couldn't even charge the driver with speeding or dangerous driving, and had no reason to breathalyse him. Presumably the flight of an empty lorry from the scene was just a cover to enable the real get-away vehicle to escape. They let them go with a caution about wasting police time.

Half an hour later the next report came in, from Hendon. A second lorry had been overtaken. P54 VRX. It had driven north up Charing Cross Road and Tottenham Court Road, through Hampstead and Golders Green to Hendon. It too was totally empty. No speeding, no traffic offence, no rudeness to the police. Names and addresses taken; dismissed with a caution. Prior added the details to his file.

He had made it clear that he wanted the lion at all costs: anything else was a distraction. Through the months of footling investigation of petty annoyances – the drama of the colours, the meaningless symbolism, the climax of the wedding and the infuriating attitude of the three principal witnesses – the one thing that would redeem all that wasted time and energy would be the recovery of the lion. That was all that mattered now. That alone – solid, tangible, weighty, iconic – would redeem his career and turn the whole sorry business into a triumph.

Five o'clock came. He was not going home now. He would see this through. News of the other lorries would come in soon. The first two had been easily found. Kilbride had said that they were not intending to steal the lion and would return it in due time. They had made their point, they had got their publicity. If they were such respectable Christians – he could not think of the phrase without a sarcastic sneer – they would do what they said. They were not criminals. They were nutters.

Six o'clock. Seven. Seven-thirty. Boredom alternated with suspense. Prior tried to get on with other work but could not concentrate. He sent out for a take-away. A skeleton staff manned his office, playing cards. At nine-thirty Prior gave up. He was dog-tired. He went home, leaving strict orders to call him if anything came up, at any hour of the night.

Redcliffe Gardens was not a haven of marital bliss that night. A phone call at 2 a.m. on Sunday morning did little to soothe his shattered nerves.

'The third lorry. A49 AUD. Yes sir, at Chalfont St Giles. Bucks. Pretty little place... no, sir. Why so late? Well, sir, it must have holed up in some garage or warehouse, then started again in the night, just to put us off the scent... Must have gone out on the M40... Yes, near Beaconsfield. Chalfont St... No, sir, absolutely empty. So we're bound to get the right one now... Yes, sir, we will. Immediately.'

Prior slept fitfully for four hours, lions and lorries pounding through his dreams, tossing and turning. His wife sought refuge in the spare bedroom. He rose early and was back at his desk by seven. He ordered coffee and a toasted sandwich, switched on the TV news, and thumbed through the papers. The phone was silent. There was no word yet of the missing lorry.

The Sunday papers had not had such a field-day since the turn of the new millennium. Archive pictures of Sir Edwin Landseer's lions featured on every front page, together with pictures of the gaping blank where one of them was not. The story of the lorries and the capture of the first two, with pictures, were related. The tabloids front-paged the beautiful Cordelia, relegating Sir Edwin's creation to an inset photo. Pages of circumstantial detail and endless speculation followed in all the papers and was hungrily pursued by breakfast TV and chat-show hosts. It was the talk of all London, the whole country and the media around the world. It was, after all, the silly season. The PM was relieved that Parliament was in recess and he would not have to face derisive taunts and barracking at Prime Minister's Questions.

News of the fourth lorry did not come in till midday, by which time Prior's shirt was a wet rag, and his eyes were beginning to droop, after a gruelling day and a broken night. At last the phone rang. He grabbed it with a sweaty hand.

'Lorry found, sir, registration H 262 RXO. Route taken, Whitehall, Westminster Bridge, then turned east, Southwark, Greenwich, Woolwich, Dartford... nearly at Gravesend when we caught it. Must have hidden under cover all night and only showed this morning. We're holding the driver. We'll bring him in straight away.'

Prior's heart was pounding. 'Well done. Good work. And the lion?'

'No sir, no sign of it. Lorry empty. They must have dumped it somewhere, but they're not talking. I'll bring them in.'

For a few moments Prior swayed, slumped head in hand,

the office swirled round him, everything went black. No lion. Gravesend: the grim name seemed symbolic. Was it the end of the quest? Was the enquiry dead and buried? He battled with himself.

Had he really been naïve enough to imagine that it would still be sitting quietly in the fourth truck? Does the road wind uphill all the way? Yes, to the bloody end, he misquoted silently. He would get them. He would nail this freaking monster raving loony mob! He would find his bloody lion. Nothing else mattered.

CHAPTER 22

Amanda Griggs lay on her bed in her small flat in Bethnal Green, as she did every night, gazing at the lights of cars from below raking the thin curtains and swinging across the ceiling. She was in a strange turmoil. It was difficult to sleep.

To begin with, she was exhausted, but the exhaustion went together with a sense of happy triumph. She really had come out on top and looked forward with a glow of anticipation to seeing her own report in the morning edition. She knew that her keenness, her willingness to work long hours, her dedication to the job, were bettering her career. The lion story was not yet finished and she was hungry for more. She would pursue the story to the end. That meant another early start tomorrow. She was ready for this, but it made it more difficult to sleep now.

She was also, as always, restless for a man. But this time, it was not just to share her bed but to share the story, to have someone who would double the pleasure of the chase by rejoicing with her. At the moment there was no one.

And today, for the first time, Amanda found herself stirred with altogether new thoughts and feelings, keeping her awake. A new level of existence seemed to be opening up beneath the habitual rush of work, the routine of commuter life, the craving for money, the round of trivial entertainment, the lure of drink and drugs, the mind-numbing beat of popular music and the hunt for short-lived affairs. It was the beginning of the discovery of herself. It was like an archaeologist digging ever deeper and finding a new layer of history, evidence of an older civilisation undreamt of before. And it had been triggered by what she had seen of Antony, Malcolm and Cordelia. Something of their spirit had communicated itself to her.

Amanda had had no chance to interview them personally before or during the wedding; afterwards they were surrounded by jostling crowds on their way to Charing Cross and the arrests followed. She knew if would be impossible to get at them while in custody; she could only hope that they might be bailed later and she would have her chance. She was determined to be on the spot when that moment came.

Amanda eyed almost any man of her own age as a potential sexual partner: Malcolm Romney was pleasant-looking enough in a rugged sort of way, and Antony Kilbride was strikingly handsome. Yet never for a moment did she imagine flirting with either of them. She was drawn to them in a different way. She found only a kind of jealousy, an admiration coupled with an intense longing for the qualities she lacked but saw in them. All three shared it. Her journalistic mind sought the right words. Poise. Serenity. Calm. Self-control. Inner-peace. Charisma. Love. And if any of those descriptions seemed too solemn and portentous, the sense of fun the three shared came to the fore, a sense of humour that embraced everyone and hurt no one. The life Amanda sensed in the wedding party seemed to show a glimpse of life at its best, life in its fullness, life as it was meant to be. For the first time in her adult existence she questioned her own philosophy, her ambitions, her very personality. Her brimming self-confidence was dented for the first time in years. She was thinking furiously, and the turmoil of impressions the day had made swirled in her mind.

As the last car parked in the narrow street outside and switched off its headlights at 1 a.m., fitful sleep came at last.

CHAPTER 23

Prior took the rest of Sunday off. Any significant developments were to be reported to him immediately, but meanwhile he forced himself to relax. For twelve hours he tried to switch off and put the whole thing out of his mind. He felt he wanted to do nothing more than watch a video of *Mary Poppins* or feed the ducks in St James's Park, metaphorically speaking. His efforts were not a success. Wherever he went, whenever he switched on the television or radio, he could not avoid some aspect of the same story: a zany wedding in Trafalgar Square and the loss of a bronze lion. He took his wife to Kew and tried to take an interest in *Indigofera dielsiana*, *Heliotropium arborescens* and *Ligularia przewalskii*, with limited success. Colours of the rainbow assaulted him wherever he went. In the evening a nice escapist movie was what he wanted, but the only one on offer seemed to be a repeat of *The Italian Job*, not the kind of thing to soothe his nerves. He left his wife happily watching, went to his study, and began jotting down ideas for the interview on the next day. He wanted to be one jump ahead. At least he started from a base of knowledge. He was dealing with some smart arses. They seemed to be cheeking the police at every turn, but with a veneer of politeness and respectability that made it very hard to pin anything on them.

Monday morning came. Prior started with Cordelia. A mistake, perhaps. She looked no worse for wear from a night in the cells. She was radiantly happy, stunningly beautiful. That was a distraction from the start. He switched on the tape.

'Interview with Cordelia Romney, Monday, 25 July, 9.05 a.m. Do you want to call a lawyer?'

'No thank you.'

'Were you involved in a plot to steal a lion from Trafalgar Square?'

'Yes, but we don't regard it as stealing. We have promised to restore it in due time.'

Prior snorted with contempt. 'I think you'll find the law takes a different view. Perhaps that's why you don't want a lawyer. I think you'll find that every other person in England regards it as theft. It is a serious offence. You seem to take it very lightly.'

'No, Inspector, we take it extremely seriously. We are concerned with the theft of our Christian heritage. That's something far, far more important.'

'Tell me more. What is it you're so concerned about?'

'It will sound rather boring to you, I'm sure. You've probably heard the same things over and over again: promiscuous sex, abortion on demand, easy divorce and remarriage and the resulting trauma for children, neglect of children, abuse of children – that's for a start. We're concerned for marriage, true marriage, with all it implies.'

'My dear young lady,' Prior adopted a fatherly tone, focusing on just one part of Cordelia's answer, 'we are living in the twenty-first century. You seem to be living in the past! You forget that the law on marriage has changed considerably, even in your lifetime.'

'Ah, law. Yes, that's the root of the problem. I'm afraid our understanding of it is very different. Modern laws are shaped by popular trends. We are concerned with another sort of law. We believe in universal principles. I don't expect you to agree.'

'Universal? Ah, I suppose you are thinking of the Universal Declaration of Human Rights,' said Prior with a contemptuous snort. He had not much time for the world on the other side of the English Channel.

'No, Inspector,' Cordelia smiled her sweetest smile. 'I am thinking of the law of God.'

Prior's frustration was expressed in the way he sighed and shrugged, turning a glance to the ceiling as if it would offer some sympathy for the trials of the police.

Cordelia pressed her advantage.

'We are a democracy, and we thank our God for that. That means we have the opportunity to change things. Short-term relationships are not the way we are made to be. Children with multiple parents – how can that be right? Most people just accept it as a fact of life: we don't. We believe that things can change. We believe in marriage as God intended it to be.'

Prior took the usual police line. He had been curious to know what made Cordelia tick, but that was enough. Private views on morality were irrelevant. Subconsciously he realised that she was getting close to the bone; his own daughter's messy divorce, his grandchildren's painful bewilderment, were in the back of his mind. He steered the talk away.

'All very interesting. You are entitled to your views, but let's stick to the point.

'We are concerned with a major public outrage. The theft of a national treasure; blatant larceny, involving major disruption in a public space; thousands of police man-hours wasted. I can assure you—'

'Outrage?' Cordelia's voice cut in, and this time it was edged with steel. Her eyes blazed. She was perfectly in control of herself but her real anger was apparent.

'Outrage, inspector? The temporary removal of a statue? Our priorities are certainly different. Rising truancy in schools, and no respect for teachers: that is an outrage. Bullying, teenage sex, drug abuse, under-age drinking, child obesity, street crime, vandalism, car theft, drink-driving, internet pornography – these are the things we are concerned about, the things the government seems helpless to control, the things, excuse me for being blunt, the police can't handle. We are disgusted at child prostitution, the exploitation of immigrants and slave labour. Our society is totally decadent but politicians don't seem to care. Even worse than all this is our parochialism, our cynical selfishness; we plunder the world for our own wealth and let millions starve. These things are the real outrage. That is why we've done what we've done.'

Cordelia angry was a sight to see. Prior was so fascinated that he let the catalogue run on while he marvelled at her moral indignation. The earthy saintliness of Joan of Arc, the crusading vigour of Mary Whitehouse, the beauty of Helen of Troy.

'All right, all right, I understand. I see your point.' He was concerned to propitiate her. He smiled. It came very close to flirting. 'That's good. Fine. I think we agree on most things. We have the same goals. But we don't break the law to achieve them.' And he decided a fatherly lecture was the best approach. The trouble was that he couldn't argue without lapsing into platitude.

'You're moral crusaders, right? You want to change society. You have your views, that's fine; we are a free democracy. Freedom of speech, excellent, but the trouble with you self-styled Christians is that you're intolerant. You don't see anyone else's point of view. You want to impose your ideals on everyone else. A bit of a killjoy attitude, wouldn't you say?'

He had fallen into a trap. For a moment he had forgotten five months of colourful display, London lifted out of its gloom by a bonanza of harmless and happy decoration, the rainbow colours that had brought a smile to the capital and drawn people together in animated speculation.

'Joy is what we believe in,' said Cordelia quietly, and everything she was demonstrated it. 'We believe in colour. We have done our bit to bring some colour to London over the last few months; surely you see that?'

A kaleidoscope of images flashed through Prior's mind. Yellow, purple, orange, red, green, blue. His mouth was open, but before anything came out of it, Cordelia continued. She was certainly in crusading mode; but her tone was quiet and persuasive; intense, but not strident.

'"*The Rainbow People of God*", that's what Archbishop Desmond Tutu called his book. That's what Christians ought to be. *The Happiest People on Earth*: That's another book title. That's our aim. "The festive instead of the workaday". That's what Pasternak said. *Dr Zhivago*, remember? "This glorious holiday from mediocrity." That's how he described Christian faith. Are you seriously accusing us of being killjoys? We have brought more colour to London than the Notting Hill Carnival.'

I ask the questions, thought Prior. The good old police cliché surfaced in his mind. The trouble was, he was enjoying this girl's feisty eloquence too much. He must get a grip on himself. Sarcasm came to his aid as usual.

'Thank you, but I ask the questions. We can do without the literary lecture. Let's get back to basics. Where is the lion?'

It was bound to come back to this, and Cordelia was quite prepared.

'I don't want to tell you. I can assure you that it is safe. It will not leave the country, and it will be restored on a certain date.'

'When?'

'I don't know. I asked not to be told. I think a date has been agreed, and Mr Kilbride knows.'

'Did you have any honeymoon plans?'

'Nothing booked. We were going to go to the Essex coast for a few days, camping, birdwatching. But we knew it might have to be postponed.'

'A train from Charing Cross to Essex? You don't know London very well, do you?' He was desperate to catch

Cordelia lying somewhere. But as soon as he had said it, he knew he had made a slip.

'Tube to Liverpool Street, then a train.' It was like them, thought Prior: no wedding car, public transport. They were out to act as publicly as possible.

'So you anticipated being arrested?'

'Yes, of course. We were quite prepared for it.'

'Yes, I can see that. You enjoy being a martyr.' And a very pretty one too, was in his mind to say, but he stopped himself just in time. 'I will be questioning you again' – the policeman in him worked by routine; the male in him gloated over the prospect – 'when we have further evidence.' He had in mind the questioning of Malcolm Romney and further investigation of the four lorries. 'Interview ends, 9.37 a.m.'

Cordelia was taken back to the cell where she embraced her beloved.

'We two alone will sing like birds i' th' cage,' he said.

'Oh yes, and we'll wear out in a wall'd prison, packs and sects of great ones that ebb and flow by th' moon,' she whispered in return, as if she were the first person in the world to say it.

CHAPTER 24

Lion hunting as a sport is no doubt almost as old as man. There is a unique thrill, an all-consuming passion, in tracking and capturing the king of beasts, which must have been immortalised in story, song and art in many cultures through the ages. That passion now took hold of Prior. He felt as if his whole career had led up to this point. It was his destiny to find and restore the lion. Cordelia had said that the lion would be returned on a certain date. He was not content with that. He was set on getting at the truth, finding and restoring the lion, not waiting passively for the crazy gang to bring it back in their own time. He was in fighting mode now; they had won round after round; the knock-out must be his.

Kilbride was interviewed again. He appeared to be the ringleader of the plot. Prior was determined to be brisk. He was going to avoid a sermon at all costs. There was only one thought in his mind: he must discover the whereabouts of the lion.

'Interview with Antony Kilbride, Monday, 25 July, 11 a.m. Do you want to call a lawyer?'

'No thank you.'

Prior began with a series of unimportant enquiries. They would probably reveal nothing about the lion but they teased his curiosity, and he battered Antony with questions in a show of painstaking thoroughness, as if no detail was too small to be of significance to an acute mind.

'This series of colour incidents. What was the point of it?'

'To bring joy to Londoners.'

'That sounds rather trivial. I thought you were mounting a serious moral crusade.'

'Serious, yes; moral, yes; crusade – no. The word is

inappropriate. We are concerned to restore Christian values, but we won't have anyone accusing us of being killjoys. Joy is our real aim. We don't call joy trivial.'

'Were you reproducing the colours of the rainbow?'

'Yes.'

'Why did you not introduce them in order?'

'Too obvious. After the first two or three people would have known what was coming next. We wanted an element of surprise.'

'There are seven. Why only six?'

'We reckon that violet and indigo are too close. Most people wouldn't distinguish them.'

'They occurred in a monthly cycle. Was that deliberate?'

'Yes.'

'But very irregularly spaced. Why?'

'We thought the first of the month each time would be boringly predictable. Joy can't be programmed. We wanted to keep people guessing.'

'How did you introduce purple into the water?'

Antony explained the technical details. Malcolm, as a civil engineer, and some of his colleagues, had worked out the method.

'Why did you presume to bother the Prime Minister with your idiotic messages?'

'He is the head of our democratic system. We wanted to alert the attention of government, as well as the public.'

'How did you select streets to send the red letters to?'

'Almost at random. Of course they all had red in the name. And roughly north, south, east and west. Of course we would have liked to send one to every house in London...'

'A red letter was sent to the Prime Minister from Budleigh Salterton. Why?'

'One of our friends happened to be going on holiday there. Nice place. Red cliffs. A fine view over Lyme Bay from West Down Beacon...'

'Yes, yes. Stick to the point, please. Were the colour incidents intended to be linked to the removal of the lion?'

'Yes. An innocent joke, we thought. Also a kind of warning of what was to come. That was the reason for the lion theme each time.'

'Quite. Of course we realised there was some significance in that very early on,' Prior exaggerated, sneakily claiming credit with the ambiguous and regal 'we.' Hicks was not present at the interview.

'Why were flowers sent to the Queen?'

This time the answer was unexpected. 'We admire her.'

'And?'

'Well, obviously blue day was a climax, as you will have realised. So we went one better than the Prime Minister.'

'So let's come to the lion. You and your colleagues deliberately removed it. A big operation for amateurs.' Prior introduced a note of grudging admiration into the dialogue.

'Not entirely amateurs,' Antony returned. 'Romney is an engineer, and he had colleagues.'

'No doubt. I shall require names and addresses from you.'

'Of course. We can supply them. We have nothing to hide. Everyone involved is willing to be questioned.'

Prior found this intensely irritating. Kilbride was taking the initiative, almost engineering the interview to make the police look ridiculous, while keeping up a front of studied politeness. Both of them envisaged a string of forty witnesses lining up voluntarily to be questioned, appearing to cooperate while wasting a massive amount of time and resources. Prior grimly returned to his battery of questions.

'So Romney masterminded the theft of the lion?'

'On the technical side, yes. It took a lot of skill and expertise.'

'And time,' snorted Prior. 'You took a hell of a risk.'

'That's why we needed a big distraction, and the colour idea developed.'

'The "cleaning and maintenance" racket was a bit of cheek. You were damned lucky to get away with that for weeks on end.'

'I believe stranger things have happened on the streets of London,' replied Antony. 'Look at all the graffiti along the railway lines. Lettering six foot high. Going on for miles. That takes some doing.'

Prior plodded on with his questions. 'Four large lorries were seen leaving Trafalgar Square at the time of the theft. Why four?'

'We thought it would cause a diversion, giving us more time to conceal the lion.'

'Caused an obstruction, I think you'll find. Obstructing the police. A very serious offence,' said Prior heavily, mentally hammering another nail into the case for the prosecution. 'I think you'll find the court will regard that as very serious indeed.'

Antony remained silent, letting Prior enjoy his sense of power. He moved on to the crunch question.

'You say you know where the lion is, your colleagues are holding it somewhere, and they will give it up on a certain date?'

'Yes.'

'What date?'

'August 29.'

'A bank holiday.'

'Yes.'

'You certainly like your publicity. Where and how will it be returned?'

'It will be restored to its original position, without any damage.'

'Where is it now?'

Kilbride knew, of course, that the question would come. He was prepared. His answer was strange.

'It is where no one is likely to find it. I know you're concerned about wasting police time. I am too. I assure you, it would be a waste of time to look for it. It has sunk without trace. It will be restored to its original position when I have said.'

Kilbride's cool self-possession infuriated Prior. His tolerant style of questioning ended abruptly. He overreacted.

'You'd better watch your language. Assuming to advise the police is extremely offensive. You will find your insolent attitude will tell against you in court. I can assure you the law will regard what you have done with extreme severity.'

Antony let the tide of pompous blather wash over him. He was careful not to allow himself the ghost of a smile.

And – as Prior could think of nothing more to say – 'I will be calling you again. Interview ends, 11.35 a.m.'

Antony was taken back to his cell. Prior returned to his office, his mood getting darker and darker. Where was that bloody lion? His thoughts tormented him because he knew it was somewhere in London or the Home Counties, but could think of no way of locating it. Hendon, Peckham, Gravesend and Chalfont St Puking Giles; north, south, east, west; somewhere between those points and central London there was a large garage, shed or warehouse containing the pompous bit of Victorian sculpture he had set his heart on.

But he soon realised he was in a cleft stick. The theft was clearly a crime – three of the culprits were in custody and would face trial – but in fact the loss of the lion harmed nobody. To search each of the four routes would be possible, but it would take a massive police operation on the scale of the hunt for a child murderer; where no danger to anyone was involved, that could not be justified. His thoughts twisted and turned but found no way out. He could do nothing but wait for 29 August. The crazy gang seemed to have won every trick. He was defeated. All he could do was promise himself that he would make it hot for them at the trial. He would see these cocky self-styled Christians banged up for as long as possible.

CHAPTER 25

Prior's interview with Malcolm Romney took a different line. He had worked out his strategy very carefully beforehand. He had decided to question him on two points only, two widely different points. On the first point, the technicality of the various incidents, he maintained a disarmingly cool front, a friendly approach, an almost directly admitted admiration for the technical skill of Malcolm and his associates.

He felt on equal terms. With Antony, a member of the clergy, he had felt ill at ease; now he was dealing with a practical man, a technician, and he felt they were on common ground.

'You and your associates have perpetrated a series of six anti-social actions in London over the past six months. Were you personally involved in all of them?'

'I would question the word anti-social. Social, perhaps: they were designed to bring people together, to make people happy, to make people laugh. But yes, I was personally involved in the idea right from the start, though my wife was the main inspiration behind the plan.'

'The yellow decorations, for example. You had a hand in that?'

'It was a big operation, as you realise. There were over a hundred of us involved all together. I did my bit with the rest.'

'But you took a leading part in at least one incident?'

'Oh yes. The purple water. That was my particular job, naturally.' Malcolm's attitude was matter-of-fact, almost sunny; the confident openness of a man with nothing to hide. Irritation began to creep into Prior's response.

'Yes, the Water Board will be making their own inquiries. That will probably be the subject of a separate prosecution,' he said, mentally rubbing his hands. 'Tell me about it.'

'About the water?'

'Yes please. I want to know how you did it. The technical details.'

And for the next ten minutes, Malcolm told him. He told the story straight. He was careful not to allow any hint of sarcasm or ridicule. He was one working man sharing his expertise with another, and Prior was genuinely interested in the method. His admiration for the technical skill of the group of engineers, their painstaking attention to detail, their meticulous timing, was quite sincere. All the more cunning, he thought inwardly, was the sudden switch to his second line of questioning. He had planned it beforehand. He would catch Romney totally off his guard and trap him into an incriminating admission. But he had underestimated his opponent.

'What do you think of Muslims?'

Ever since the wedding in the Square the previous Saturday, when Prior had realised that the crazy gang were in fact fundamentalist Christians, he had been especially aware of the dangers of religious hatred. London had been on edge for a long time. The terrorist threat had been well recognised years before the suicide bombings of the 7 July 2005. The growth of militant Islam was an ever-present thorn in the flesh of the police. Legislation to curb racial hatred, and religious hatred, was high on the political agenda. The police walked a tightrope of political correctness, aware of the dangers of discrimination. They had the impossible task of maintaining public order, well knowing the public outcry that followed if their stop-and-search methods could be seen as targeting those of Asian appearance. Relations between Christians and Muslims were a key area of tension, and British Christians, normally so tolerant as to be lukewarm about their own faith, were now beginning to reassert their identity.

Now, Prior had reasoned, these colour-crazy, so-called born-again Christians were just the kind of people to aggravate an already tense religious situation. They were the equivalent of the religious right in America: the moral majority. He regarded it as his public duty to detect and suppress any vestige of Anti-Muslim feeling. He also inwardly gloated that this was another nail he could hammer home in his determination to get the better of these suave middle-class religious cranks with their infuriating coolness. But Malcolm was not to be thrown. He handled the change of tack with admirable calm. His reply was not glib and it was certainly not meant to be funny. He paused for a few seconds and then replied with total sincerity.

'What do you think of Muslims?'

'We love them.'

It was Prior who was thrown off balance. The wildly improbable answer took him by surprise and he stared in confusion for several seconds. Although the rigid code of political correctness prevented him from expressing such thoughts, Asians, immigrants and Islamic extremists had long been docketed in his mind as the enemy.

He played for time.

'Explain what you mean by that.'

Malcolm was only too glad to enlarge upon his beliefs. He too, like Cordelia and Antony before him, now had the chance to fly the flag. This was the outcome of the whole plan, the reason for courting maximum publicity. The opportunity to witness was the foreseen and welcomed purpose of the whole project.

'We try to follow Jesus. It's as simple as that. He taught love of God and love of people, love of enemies, forgiveness and reconciliation. We believe his voice needs to be heard in

Britain today. We believe the vicious circle of violence in our society needs to be broken. We believe hatred can only be banished by love. We believe—'

Prior found this line of thought so ridiculous that he began to feel himself on firmer ground. He recovered his habitual cynicism. He laughed.

'Well, well, well. I never thought I'd hear that sort of language in the twenty-first century. We seem to be back in the days of the hippies. Flower-power, all you need is love – Is that what it's all about? I never heard such idealistic rubbish. How naïve can you get?'

But Malcolm was not to be wrong-footed so easily.

'I agree with you, Inspector. If it was just talk, you'd be right. But it's not. That's why we concentrate on individuals. Antony Kilbride's church in the City is a meeting place for Muslims and Christians. We don't agree with each other. We debate. We argue! But we try to treat people as people. They are our friends. We try to help them and we try to learn from them. We love them; yes, I don't see why we should be ashamed of that word. We love them because God loves them as he loves us. It's nothing airy-fairy; it's the way of Jesus. It's down to earth, it's real. It's more important than anything else. That's why we've done what we've done.'

'Suicide bombers? Those who kill innocent people – women and children? You love them?' Prior's tone was hard, totally unbelieving.

Again Malcolm paused and reflected; his answer had the ring of sincerity. 'Yes. We make an effort to love them. We hate what they do; we hate the violence; we hate the crime; we hate the false philosophy that prompts them to do it, but we can't hate the men themselves. They are people. We don't see any other way to get back to normality.'

Prior had heard enough. His head was whirling. His concern was always the immediate task. He was not used to trying to solve the long term problems of society. He reverted to heavy sarcasm.

'Normality is certainly what we need. I hope you and your misguided friends will remember that. Stealing national treasures is not normality; wasting countless hours of valuable police time is not normality. I shall be speaking to you again. In future, I would advise you to confine yourself to answering questions put to you. I can assure you preaching will not go down well in front of a magistrate. Interview ends...' and he spoke the date and time into the tape recorder. Malcolm meekly followed the police escort back to his cell.

CHAPTER 26

The next day, Tuesday, Malcolm, Cordelia and Antony were released on bail. It had been planned. The whole group of their friends who had been at the wedding shared the cost. The timing again was carefully planned. It had been agreed beforehand that the three should have a chance to witness to the police at the preliminary interviews, and then bailed so that they would be able to talk to the press. Prior foresaw this but could find no legal reason for denying bail. The offer of bail came late on the Tuesday afternoon, timed so that the story would hit the papers on Wednesday morning.

Cordelia coming out of prison was like the sun bursting through clouds. Marcus was ready with his camera among the crowd of other press photographers. His shot of her was one of the best in his career; he fell in love with it and had it framed and hung on his wall afterwards. It almost filled the front page of his paper, under the banner headline 'THE LION QUEEN', and put the page-three girl in the shade.

Cordelia, Malcolm and Antony made the most of their opportunity, and their Christian moral arguments shook London the next day. They were certainly letting their light shine before men.

The morning paper headline writers had a bonanza:

'RELEASE OF THE LION TAMERS';

'LION SNATCHERS OUT OF JAIL';

'BAIL FOR THE THREE MUSKETEERS';

'TRAFALGAR TRIO BAILED';

'NEW BATTLE OF TRAFALGAR';

'ENGLAND EXPECTS RETURN OF LION';
'BORN AGAIN: THREE CHRISTIANS BAILED'.

When the three were released it was a full twenty minutes before the crowds began to disperse. The last camera had flashed, and the journalists had squeezed everything they could from the story – all but one. Marcus rushed back to the office with his pictures, but Amanda remained. She stepped up to Malcolm and Cordelia.

'Can I buy you a drink?'

Her seriousness appealed to them. Malcolm smiled and looked at Cordelia, who nodded agreement.

'Thanks. That would be good. As long as it's not water. Antony?'

'I need to get home,' said Antony. 'Things to do. I'll leave you to it. See you tomorrow evening after work?'

They arranged to meet, Antony disappeared into the crowd and the three looked for a pub. Amanda strode ahead and led the way to a pub she knew off Fleet Street. It was near one of those narrow lanes tucked away from the main thoroughfares of the City of London; it was called Red Lion Court. She thought it a tremendous joke.

At the end of two hours Amanda found herself mentally and spiritually exhausted. Later, at the end of the year, she looked back with thankfulness on a turning point in her life, an eye-opening experience, an encounter with reality. She had staged the interview with the sublime assurance of a twenty-four-year-old, the pushiness of a career journalist, the confidence of a fast-track professional. She soon found the tables beginning to turn. 'I ask the questions' was the unwritten code of the reporter, as well as of the police, but in a short time the questions were coming the other way, and questions that got beneath her tough professional skin. Harry had commissioned her to spend time on the case, to blow it up into a major feature, not just a news item. She was prepared to spend time on the job.

By the laws of social behaviour the act of ordering drinks should have put Amanda in the driving seat; she was host; she could dictate the conversation. It did not work out like that. The world of hard facts soon gave way to meanings and motives, ideas and ideals. An hour went by; the dialogue showed no signs of ending. Cordelia suggested eating together, and offered to pay. They moved to the bar to order. The initiative had subtly changed.

Amanda went through all the practical questions that she had jotted down to ask. It was a long list, the same questions that had arisen in the police interviews, eliciting the same answers. What was the point of the colour days? Why the rainbow? Why the Prime Minister? Why Budleigh Salterton? Was there a connection between the colours and the lion? Did they remove the lion? Why a wedding in public? Why four lorries? And of course, where is the lion now? This last point Amanda had carefully prepared, not in a direct form, but through several indirect trick questions aimed at getting at this all-important fact. The passion of the lion hunt was as strong in her as in Prior, but she got no further than he had done.

It was on the question of motive that she began to slide off her interviewer's perch and become more vulnerable. As all London was asking, she had to ask: what was the point of it all? Was it simply fun? A gigantic and rather expensive hoax? Why were they willing to risk prosecution for the theft of the lion? What did it all mean?

In answer, Malcolm put down his glass, leaned his arms on the table, and looked Amanda full in the eyes.

'What is your "lion"?' he asked quietly.

'My lion?'

'Yes. The lion is a symbol. I suppose Nelson's lions are a symbol of pride in the Empire. Not something we value much today. For us, the lion is the symbol of something very much greater: the king – and I don't mean Elvis Presley. The person at the centre of history. The person who made us count the years backwards, divided history into BC and AD. The lion of the tribe of Judah. Jesus Christ.'

'Fine, fine.' Amanda was quite as prepared to report the ideas of religious freaks as anything else. In fact, the more outlandish, the better the story. She would get all the juicy details, all the weird language, all the crazy beliefs and practises of these nutters. She had the usual atheist slant of modern youth.

'Fine. Do go on. Tell me more.'

'You haven't answered my question,' returned Malcolm politely.

I ask the questions, thought Amanda automatically; but didn't say it.

'Sorry? What question?'

'What is your "lion"?'

'I don't follow.'

'The lion represents everything we think most important, everything we love, our passion, the one over-riding reality in our lives. So what is yours? If that's too personal, you don't have to answer, but you won't understand our answer unless you can see it that way.'

Amanda, inwardly baffled, kept her cool exterior. What was of supreme importance to her at the moment? She tried desperately to find something. A wildly expensive outfit she had seen in Whistles? A holiday in Biarritz? A new flat? A step up the property ladder from her squalid pad in Bethnal Green? An upward move in her career? A boy? Yes, a boy was first on the list. She was between boyfriends, and that came first. But she was not going to be pinned down.

'Human relationships,' she replied with a sweet smile. 'People.' Well, it was not a lie. It covered the truth nicely and presented her as a warm, caring person.

'So you're a humanist,' Cordelia took up the dialogue.

'Well, er, I never thought of myself like that... but, yes, I suppose that's what I am.'

'That's great. So are we!'

'But I thought... I don't see—'

'Christians are humanists, the best kind of humanists. We believe in someone who was a model of what humanity should be. "The man, Christ Jesus", the Bible calls him. People are important. It's good we agree on that.'

The approach that bracketed Amanda together with these born-again weirdos was not at all to her liking. She was concerned to distance herself from them, to maintain her cool objectivity. Yet inwardly something was stirring. Was a new boyfriend the summit of her desires? Perhaps there was more to life. As the talk went on she became gradually less hostile, less professional, more willing to talk person to person, more willing to listen. Perhaps these people had something after all.

'Pudding?' said Malcolm, getting up. 'On me. What will you have?'

'Oh, er, nothing for me thanks,' Amanda answered, ever conscious of her figure. 'Coffee would be nice.' A great concession. She could have swept away with journalistic self-importance and cut the debate short; but there was still time to get her story in for the morning edition, and she was now becoming truly engaged. 'Human relations', she had said airily. Now she was relating, listening, questioning, pondering. The talk became increasingly personal and yet increasingly relaxed. Amanda even found herself laughing with them, and heads turned at nearby tables. These people might or might not be humanists, but they were certainly human.

When after two hours they got up to go, Amanda amazed herself by asking for another date to continue the discussion, a time when they could again relax and talk without her reporter's notebook. She was intrigued, puzzled and thirsty to know more. The protective armour of her self-sufficiency had been gently dinted, her horizons subtly expanded. What was her 'lion'? Had she no passion worthy of her whole devotion? It seemed as if her whole life was being slowly turned around. They fixed a day at the end of August.

'After D-Day!' Amanda grinned.

'Yes,' said Cordelia, 'or shall we call it L-Day?'

As they emerged into Fleet Street Amanda looked up at the sign on the corner of the narrow alley. Red Lion Court. She smiled.

Harry praised Amanda's coverage of the incident and devoted plenty of space to it in the Wednesday morning edition. She pulled out all the stops of her journalistic prose, garnishing the story with quips and puns, sailing as close to the edge of truth as she dared. This was her big moment. She basked in glory. She had not included in her report the words 'salvation', 'love', 'atonement', 'sin', 'holiness' or 'glory'; but for that night and for many nights to come they circled in her mind.

CHAPTER 27

The capital buzzed with excitement as the weeks went on. The expected return of the lion was a talking point in trains and buses, pubs, restaurants and offices across the land. The foreign press took up the story in a big way. Japanese tourists booked last-minute flights to London to be there for the great day.

Prior, shoulders sagging with disgust at the whole wearisome business, ordered a modified police presence in the Square for Bank Holiday Monday, with emergency plans in reserve in case of unforeseen trouble. He owned failure and contented himself with the prospect of turning up the heat when he came to give evidence at the trial. The strange phrase Antony had used – 'sunk without trace' – nagged him, but still provided no clue. Could it possibly be that the lion was literally submerged? That it was hidden, not in the wilds of outer London, but at the bottom of the Thames? Why on earth should anyone go to that sort of trouble and expense? From the first day of the whole enquiry months before to this bizarre conclusion he owned himself baffled. It was small consolation to think that neither Hicks nor anyone else had done any better. The crazy gang had won their ridiculous game. But they would pay for it.

Cordelia went back to her drawing board and Malcolm to his desk, where their colleagues regarded them with a certain awestruck admiration, and life was as normal as could be till the end of August, though Malcolm was well aware of the impending internal inquiry that was bound to follow his actions.

Trafalgar Square was alive with excitement from first light on 29 August, Bank Holiday Monday. Crowds had begun to gather overnight, as if for a royal occasion.

It soon appeared that the day was to be a day of colour and celebration, outstripping the previous days of colour and even the wedding. The rolls of blue carpet appeared again, the sound equipment was set up, together with a large screen and projector. The same band moved onto the site and began playing as soon as the first rays of the sun struck Nelson on his perch. From all corners of the Square costers' barrows were wheeled in, laden with flowers, which were distributed around the plaza, and this time they were all the colours of the rainbow; there were scarlet, orange and yellow roses; blue delphiniums and hydrangeas; red carnations, geraniums and salvias; yellow gladioli, dahlias, chrysanthemums; purple orchids, larkspurs, pansies, petunias; orange marigolds and calendulas; all in riotous confusion, and set off by masses of greenery. Kew Gardens and the Chelsea Flower Show seemed to have met in Trafalgar Square. A catalogue of summer beauty from aconite to zinnia put the whole concourse in holiday mood.

As morning wore on and the day brightened, families with children joined the crowds. Basketfuls of favours were handed around – balloons, paper streamers, party poppers, silly string, banners, flags, toys and sweets of all colours, as if Mary Poppins had touched the streets with her magic. The square became a fluttering, dancing, waving mass of colour. Laughing, cheering, singing, broke out in sections of the crowd. People did not seem to mind that this time the Christian message was expressed explicitly in words: The banners, flags and balloons were all printed with Biblical words. The Square that had seen so many demonstrations through the years now witnessed a message of love and joy. Ban the Bomb, Scrap the Poll Tax, Drop the Debt, Stop Hunting Now, Pensioners' Rights, Gay Rights, Animal Rights, Stop the War – these had been the slogans of past decades. The words now were not strident, and the print

was small, but it was there for all to see:
> REJOICE IN THE LORD ALWAYS.
> LOVE THE LORD YOUR GOD.
> BY GRACE YOU ARE SAVED, THROUGH FAITH.
> JESUS CHRIST, THE LIGHT OF THE WORLD.
> LOVE YOUR NEIGHBOUR.
> COME, LORD JESUS!
> THE LORD IS MY SHEPHERD.
> GOD SO LOVED THE WORLD.
> IN EVERYTHING GIVE THANKS.
> WALK IN THE SPIRIT.
> JESUS IS LORD.
> TRUST IN THE LORD WITH ALL YOUR HEART.

The police had a problem. Tough questioning in the interview room had failed to elicit the important information: how would the lion be returned? Prior reasoned: presumably it would be in one of the same four lorries. Presumably there would only be one; there would be no point in the presence of the three others this time. But which way would it come? He considered the six approaches – Pall Mall or Haymarket leading into Cockspur Street, Charing Cross Road leading into St Martin's Place, The Strand, Northumberland Avenue, Whitehall, The Mall. The last two were perhaps the most likely, he thought; the bastards were out for maximum publicity, and a broad ceremonial route would appeal to them. But Kilbride's odd phrase 'It's sunk without trace' teased his brain like a mosquito. Could they really have sunk the flaming thing in the Thames? If so, Northumberland Avenue would be the direct route. He posted a couple of men by Hungerford Bridge to watch the river.

The day moved towards noon, the crowds thickened,

spilling out into the surrounding streets. People appeared at the windows and on the rooftops of public buildings. Barelegged children splashed in the fountains; balloons let go by toddlers floated into the London sky to carry their message of a forgotten gospel to the far corners of the metropolis. The swinging mood flowed out into central London and the police waited, alert but patient, enjoying the party. The band went blithely through a repertoire of colourful tunes – 'Red Sails in the sunset', 'Yellow Ribbons', 'Blue Suede Shoes', 'Memphis Blues, 'Somewhere Over the Rainbow', 'Green Green Grass of Home', 'Joseph's Amazing Technicolour Dreamcoat'. The crowd joyfully joined in the words:

> 'I look handsome, I look smart, I am a walking work of art,
> Such a dazzling coat of many colours,
> How I love my coat of many colours...
> It was red and yellow and green and brown
> and scarlet and black and ochre and peach
> and ruby and olive and violet and fawn
> and lilac and gold and chocolate and mauve
> and cream and crimson and silver and rose
> and azure and lemon and russet and grey
> and purple and white and pink and orange and blue.'

Hicks was at Prior's elbow. The irrepressible Hicks, cocky as ever.

'Quite a sight, sir! We haven't had a rally like this since—'

'Yes, Hicks.'

'I don't see how they're gonna get through this crowd with a lorry.'

'We'll see. I've got men posted on the approach roads all around. I'm gonna stop the bloody thing way outside the area. The driver will be arrested. That'll spoil their damn party.'

'Yes, sir. Just the job. Only I just had a thought.'

It's my nemesis, thought Prior, my karma. Listening to this man's cock-eyed thoughts. I'm fated to have Hicks on my coat-tails for the rest of my life. All he said was, 'Yes?'

'Well, chief, all these guys are after is max publicity, right? They want to make a sensation. They've been spreading mayhem across London for months. Now this is the climax. They've got to go one better. This has got to be big. Well, I know what I'd do.'

'Well?'

'A helicopter, sir.'

Prior considered the idea for a long time in silence, and involuntarily gazed up at the sky. Thoughts and counter-thoughts raced in his mind. He could almost hear the racket of a chopper's wings. But only the faint drone of a passenger airliner at 6,000 feet disturbed the summer air. He grunted.

'Yes, Hicks. You may be right. So that's your job: get your telescope out and scan the fleecing sky for the rest of the day. And don't blame me if you get a stiff neck.'

It was the reaction Hicks expected. Sarcasm was the usual tone of a police officer to a junior. Nobody minded that. But inwardly he stuck to his idea, and Prior admitted to himself, though not to anyone else, that it was a possibility. He phoned Scotland Yard and told them to check local airports and report any unusual helicopter movements.

And then his stomach churned. A new thought had hit him. What if it was a terrorist attack after all? The thought was so appalling that he broke out in sweat. Another 9/11. Another 7/7. This time it would be 8/29. London was in constant fear of a terrorist incident – could this be it? Could the pathetic parade of colour days, the bluff of the ridiculous wedding, the stealing of the lion and the whole charade of so-called Christian witness, be one gigantic prelude to a cynical and ruthless bomb attack on the biggest crowd since the turn of the millennium? Perhaps it was a backlash of the evangelical right, a sort of born-again National Front.

Terrorism was carried on in the name of Islam; now so-called Christianity was fighting back. Why had he not thought of this before?

With an effort Prior controlled his reactions and remained outwardly calm, assured, commanding. He would share the thought with no one at this stage. The last thing he wanted was panic in a crowd of this size. All he could do was to send out messages to his men at intervals not to relax vigilance, to report anything suspicious, however slight, and to keep in constant touch with him. In this way the afternoon wore on, as London, and the world, waited for the return of the lion.

CHAPTER 28

Cordelia and her friends mingled with the crowd, enjoying the festival atmosphere. She seemed to have no particular role. However the lion was going to reappear, it was not her responsibility. All she did was to move slowly round the area, talking to as many people as possible, her flaming head standing out like a poppy in a wheatfield. Antony Kilbride was there too, sauntering, jostling, talking to anyone and everyone, handing out presents to children, apparently as carefree as them. Prior had identified them early on and set two men to tail them and report any suspicious movements. Malcolm was nowhere to be seen in the Square.

Amanda and Marcus were there among an army of home and foreign paparazzi, gladly giving up their Bank Holiday for the chance of a scoop. She had been in at the start, she reflected, and she would be in at the kill. She recalled the early morning call from Harry and the hunt for all things yellow back in February, and smiled. A lot had happened since then. It seemed another world.

Every now and then there was a surge at the extremities of the crowd as a vehicle approached, trying to find a way through the mob of people, and the noise of voices rose in expectancy as everyone turned in that direction, but it was always a false alarm. There was no sign of any large lorry similar to the four that had been at the wedding, and none were reported anywhere in central London. Prior found it hard to contain his anxiety, and periodically glanced up at the sky, taking care to do it when Hicks was not around. No helicopter showed.

Meanwhile the Christian message flashed gaily around the area. A huge screen had been set up, with a succession of power-point images: pictures of natural beauty, happy laughing people, children at play, dancing, the sea, mountains, sunsets, flowers. And interspersed with them were Christian messages, Bible words, simple prayers and sometimes the words of a song of worship in which people in the crowd spontaneously joined.

The plinth around Nelson's column was still partly shrouded in scaffolding and hoardings, but it was the place to which all heads were suddenly turned. Something was happening. There was an audible gasp from the sections of the crowd near enough to see, and the whole mass of people from all around the square turned towards the column. The volume of noise steadily rose, the ranks of onlookers pressed towards the centre and the media fought to make a way through to the front. But there was one pair who were in exactly the right position from the start. Amanda and Marcus were in on the action, closer than any of the others. They had been tipped off by Cordelia and sworn to secrecy.

At the foot of the column a gaping rectangular hole had appeared in the paving, and in the hole there was movement; movement as slow and steady as the turn of the London Eye on its axle, as slow as the *Mary Rose* when it was lifted from the seabed in its giant cradle. Inch by inch something was rising from the hole, a certain dark, shiny and heavy something, noiselessly lifted above the level of the paving, up and up into the sunlight, like a body from the grave. It was the lion.

A roar went up, the roar of the home crowd at the last-minute winning goal of a football match. There was no doubt what was happening. The news soon passed to the fringes of the crowd, who could not yet see the action. Cheer upon cheer went up, laughter, waving of flags, release of balloons, shooting of party poppers, squirting of silly string. Soon the shining body of the lion was high enough for all to see, standing on a wooden platform raised by some hydraulic engine underground, and in triumph was slid gently back onto its plinth. The operation had worked perfectly. Months of planning and engineering had paid off. Malcolm and a team of helpers emerged from the hole, happy but dishevelled. Malcolm, the borough engineer. Cordelia fought her way through the mass of people to embrace him.

It was at that moment that the band had its finest hour. They turned up the decibels to the maximum. The sound was heard in Covent Garden, in Soho, in Parliament Square and on the River. But the sound was neither the sugar-sweet tones of easy listening nor the raucous hammering of heavy metal. It was a majestic voice from the time of King George II, the voice of George Frederick Handel; a hymn of life restored and victory over death, calling London to the praise of the risen, conquering son, the lion of the tribe of Judah. The words appeared on the big screen and tens of thousands of voices joined in celebrating the resurrection of the lion.

'See! Jesus meets us, risen from the tomb,
lovingly he greets us, scatters fear and gloom.
Let the church with gladness hymns of triumph sing,
for her Lord is living, death has lost its sting.
Thine be the glory, risen conquering Son,
endless is the victory thou o'er death hast won.'

One person not singing was Prior. He stood helpless. There seemed nothing to do. Inwardly he felt drained. For months he had followed this ridiculous plot, always one step behind. Every movement of the police had been reactive. He had been led by the nose. Now he felt tricked, cheated, humiliated. All he could do in his rage was to snarl at Hicks, 'Still looking for helicopters, Hicks?' It was a cheap triumph to be able to prove Hicks wrong; small consolation for the fiasco that the whole affair had been. He forced himself to act professionally.

'Hicks, bring in that man. Romney, the engineer. Arrest him. Charge him with a breach of the peace, burglary, obstructing the police; anything you bloody well like.'

'Yes, sir.' The arrest was made.

Prior could not relax. He could not allow himself to think that this was the end of the story. The fear of a terrorist attack had gripped him, and even now, when the adventure of the lion seemed to be wrapped up, he was on the alert. There was still the possibility that the whole episode was a blind for something else, a massive distraction, while some genuine outrage was occurring elsewhere. His orders became terser, businesslike, aggressive. He phoned the Yard.

'I want more men. The crowd is going berserk. Anything could happen. Maintain total vigilance to the end of the day in central London. Monitor all plane movements.'

The idea of an aerial attack still haunted him. And so his colleagues at the Yard, and the Metropolitan Police, spent a tedious Bank Holiday Monday, waiting, watching, on edge, trying to pretend they were doing a vital job, but in reality getting more and more bored as nothing happened. Tourists waited patiently, shuffling nearer to the lion to take photographs, and went home tired but happy. The band packed up and left. The hot August sun began to go down, the fountains flashed, the crowds gradually dispersed, and, as after the wedding, an army of cheerful volunteers swept the whole Square clean of litter and removed all the waste. The pigeons fluttered down and pecked what they could from the ground. London returned to its predictable everyday greyness, ready for the return to work the following day. There were no helicopters, no car bombs, no vandalism, no outbreak of crime; nothing worse than the usual rowdiness when the pubs closed at the end of a Bank Holiday.

Malcolm was taken into custody, which caused him and Cordelia no surprise. They could endure more than separation for the sake of a great cause. The happiness of victory enfolded them, and though they slept apart, their sleep that night was deep and undisturbed.

CHAPTER 29

Thirty minutes can be a long time in anyone's life. In the space of thirty minutes enemies can be reconciled, contracts signed, a marriage arranged or a divorce agreed. A peace treaty might be concluded or a bomb detonated, a man employed or a woman sacked, a terminal illness diagnosed or a baby delivered. Issues of life and death could be decided in the space of half an hour.

Above the River Thames, looking down on the Royal Festival Hall on the south bank and across to the Houses of Parliament and Westminster Abbey, stands a symbol of the twenty-first century, the 135 metre-high giant observation wheel, the biggest in the world, known as the London Eye. The structure is well placed to be seen from many points in Westminster, and stands in full view of anyone walking up Victoria Street. Thirty spacious glass capsules, called gondolas, circulate so slowly that the movement is hardly noticeable. Each accommodates about twenty people, giving unrivalled all-round views of the city. The smoothness and quietness of the circular journey through space takes the traveller far above the hum and bustle of the city streets. The Eye is like a time machine, transporting one not so much back into the past or forward into the future but outside time altogether. It is like a momentary withdrawal from life. The circuit of one gondola takes thirty minutes.

It was at the London Eye that Amanda had arranged to meet with Cordelia, on Tuesday 30 August. Malcolm, as the leader of the engineering team that had managed the sinking and raising of the lion, was back in police custody, but Antony and Cordelia were free on bail, awaiting their trial. Cordelia had taken two weeks off work for what should have been her honeymoon. Amanda had asked Harry for the day off – a reasonable demand after her constant vigilance over the past months; and now that the lion story was unlikely to yield any more copy, at least until the trial of the ringleaders, Harry was happy to agree. The two girls bought their tickets and stood in line in Jubilee Gardens. It was the school holidays and the tourist season, and the queue was long, though not as long as it would have been on the previous day, the Bank Holiday.

They had plenty of time to talk, and the time was not wasted. Amanda, against all her instincts, had forced herself to leave her notebook and her cell-phone behind. It was a serious psychological struggle. She was a reporter to the fingertips; her life hitherto had been focussed on her career, and that meant one thing only: a story. Nothing mattered but getting into print. Going out without a notebook or a phone, she felt half naked. She was like a wino without a bottle, a junkie without a fix, a gambler without cash. But a deeper longing now possessed her. Partly, she admitted to herself, it was plain curiosity to know why three respectable, middle-class people had risked such a lot and given so much of their time and energy to a gigantic hoax. Partly, it was an undefined desire to come closer to the spirit that motivated them and a genuine admiration for their outlandish behaviour.

Their turn came at last, and, with twenty or so others, they boarded. Inch by inch the gondola crept upwards and they were soon above the roofs below. One by one the surrounding public buildings came into view: the Festival Hall, the National Theatre, Waterloo Station on the south bank; across the river, Big Ben and the Houses of Parliament to the left, then the Victoria Embankment backed by the government buildings of Whitehall, ships moored along the river near Charing Cross Station; and behind, the National Gallery, St Martin in the Fields and Nelson's Column, marking the Square that had been the focus of the world's press the day before. Away to their right, the spires of Wren's City churches pierced the spaces between modern office blocks, and the dome of St Paul's Cathedral dominated the skyline. Further east, they could dimly discern Tower Bridge and the city's oldest building, the Tower of London.

Though the gondola was filled with people, Amanda wanted to talk and did not let that inhibit her. Amid the chatter of others and the excited babble of children they could talk quietly without embarrassment.

'You certainly made your mark,' Amanda began, gazing down on the network of streets. 'The old place needs brightening up.'

'Yes, well, colour is my business,' Cordelia replied, keeping the tone light. She told Amanda about her job. That in itself was of interest; with the vibrant state of the housing market, interior design was a fashionable topic. Countless house make-over programmes on TV peddled the importance of good design, furnishing and decoration. It was a booming industry.

'But redecorating London? A make-over for the city? What a fantastic idea! How did it come about?'

Cordelia considered. 'Well, I can only answer that by going right back to basics, our basic beliefs. You see, there are hundreds of us who have a passionate belief in one thing. And that one thing is so important it is worth doing great things for; even crazy things.'

'You mean your religion.'

Cordelia smiled and considered. 'I don't like either of those words, actually! Religion, now: the word creates all the wrong images; RE at school; priests and rituals; shrines and temples; weird customs and festivals – Passover, Divali, Ramadan, Easter; all the externals. They are all cultural trappings. We are concerned with the inner core, the real meaning: truth.'

'You said you didn't like either of those words,' said Amanda. 'What did you mean?'

'Ah, yes, the word "your". "Your religion". "Your taste in clothes". "Your lifestyle". "Your likes and dislikes". "Your hair colour". "Your holiday plans". It implies something that you have chosen, something that is smaller than you, something you control and something that is just one part of your life: a leisure activity, a hobby. But real faith is not like that. Yes, we have made a choice; but in a way, it has chosen us. It is something so much bigger than any of us. It is universal truth.'

The widening view seemed to lend weight to her words; the meandering river with its many bridges upstream – Westminster, Vauxhall, Battersea, Chelsea; downstream, Waterloo, Tower Bridge, the docks beyond, the shipping, Greenwich, Woolwich and the estuary out to the east, where the river widened into the North Sea. All around the hazy sunshine blurred the meeting of land and sea and one could imagine the curve of the earth's surface, defining the limits of existence. Inevitably it lifted the spirits. Pettiness was rebuked. The self-centred strivings of daily life seemed to shrink and look small.

'Truth!' Amanda echoed. It was a word she recognised. 'That's just the point; I am concerned with truth – that's what a journalist does. We are passionate about truth, what really happens. But religion is just speculation; it's what people imagine. It's wishful thinking.'

Again Cordelia smiled gently. 'Really? I wish I could believe that. I don't get that impression when I open a paper. If you're honest, wouldn't you say that the mass of journalists are not concerned with truth? They are concerned with the story.'

It was a distinction Amanda had hardly considered, and she took a moment to think about it now. In her mind, truth and the story were the same thing. Searching her inmost heart, she would have to admit that Cordelia was right; but it was painful to accept it. The question haunted her for days to come.

'But what is truth, then?'

'Jesus!'

Amanda was so used to hearing the name as a swear word that she did not immediately grasp that Cordelia was giving her a serious answer.

'Yes, Jesus. Christ. Somehow he sums it all up. He is the "lion". He is what motivates us. He is our model. He is ultimate man. He is universal truth. He is real. He walked the streets, he ate fish, he wept, he loved, he sweated and died. But he is not just real: he is reality itself.'

Amanda gazed at the panoramic view, her thoughts whirling. The gondola was nearing its zenith. They were suspended between heaven and earth. The quiet was uncanny. Amanda's position struck her as rather ridiculous. Here she was, wasting her holiday, talking about religion with an enthusiast 130 feet above the River Thames in a glass globule. And yet she did not feel trapped. Curious, yes, but also excited. Cordelia's quiet certainty combined with graciousness of manner impressed her.

'The alpha and the omega,' Cordelia was saying.

'The what?'

'Well, it's a phrase from the Bible. Alpha and omega; the first and last letters of the Greek alphabet. The A to Z. That's what Christ is. He sums up everything. He is all we need to know about life. He is the truth.'

They were now at the top of the circle. There were no longer any other gondolas above them. There was an eerie sense of floating in space, of being suspended in nothingness. They paused in their conversation to scan the 360-degree panorama. The day was fine and sunny, but as so often in London, hazy; on the edges of sight the limits of the land melted into the sky. Amanda felt as if the universe, through the quiet presence beside her, was asking her a single question, waiting for a response. There was silence in heaven for half an hour.

CHAPTER 30

Amanda knew she would have to wrestle with her inner self alone. For the first time in her adult life, she was being made to think about issues beyond her own career. She resolved to take time out to think. Meanwhile, she steered the conversation onto safer ground.

'"The truth". It's a bit too philosophical for me,' she replied, though even as she said it she was uneasily aware that the response was a kind of mental laziness, an evasion. 'So you stole a three-ton lion.'

'Removed and restored,' corrected Cordelia, as she had done to the police. 'Yes. What would you have done? You see, for the past year a big group of us, a hundred or more, have had a sense that we ought to act. We are sickened by the trends of society. Casual sex is probably the root of it…'

Amanda flushed inwardly, but preserved a cool front with an effort of self-control.

'That leads to marriage breakdown,' Cordelia went on, 'or the devaluing of marriage altogether. Children grow up without a father or with two fathers. Problems at school follow – truancy, bullying, bad behaviour – and that leads on to teenage sex, binge drinking, drugs and all the rest of it. Then you get vandalism, car theft and violent crime. Another generation follows and the vicious circle goes on. We wanted to do something about it.'

'So you're the far right; the moral majority?'

'We are Christians.'

'But from the sound of it… by what you've just said…'

'Look, we decided to do something, to make a mark, to remove an icon. Greenpeace activists sail little boats in the path of oil tankers; conservationists build homes in trees.

We decided to do something big. Christians have been quiet for far too long.'

'Fine, fine. So you plan to steal a lion. But why the colours?'

'Two reasons. The practical one: we knew the lion operation would take months. It was planned to the last detail. It was like prisoners escaping from Colditz, but on a bigger scale. We had to fool the police and the local authorities, who came to inspect us, while doing the tunnelling and engineering work. So we thought a pretty large-scale distraction would be good, something to divert the press and get the police hunting on a false trail.'

'Well, it certainly worked.' Amanda's admiration was ungrudging. 'As a publicity stunt, it was fantastic, you certainly made a splash. But what was the other reason?'

'You said just now that we appeared to be the moral majority. What does the word "morality", or "moralist", mean to most people?'

'Something a bit heavy-handed, I suppose. The strong arm of the law. Something oppressive, something grim.'

'Exactly. Everything we want to avoid. We had to break the stereotype of Christians as repressive moralists, as killjoys. Joy is our creed. Jesus is joy. We believe in happiness. You know C S Lewis? He wrote the Narnia books for children. Aslan, the lion – remember? And Lewis wrote: "It is a Christian duty for everyone to be as happy as he can".'

Things fell into place in Amanda's mind. It was the essential happiness that she had seen in Antony, Malcolm and Cordelia that had impressed her. It was not brashness, not heartiness, but a quiet underlying joy that stood out in contrast to the cynicism that infected modern life like a cancer. Perhaps it was that joy that in her deepest self she admired and coveted.

'We wanted to break the negative image,' Cordelia went on. 'We wanted to bring joy to London. To make our point, yes. The loss of the lion was meant to symbolise the loss of so much that we care for in society, but the colours, the colours of the rainbow, they are not superficial. They come from the heart of God. They are embedded in the Bible story. They are part of the human psyche. They are what we need. If you've lost the joy, you've lost everything.'

Again, what emanated from Cordelia made its impression, as markedly as her flaming red hair illumined the gondola when the sun fell on it. Serenity was a part of it; quiet certainty was a part of it. But there was also a kind of love; love that manifested itself as a genuine concern for Amanda; a respect for her person; a tacit acknowledgement of her value; the loving a neighbour as oneself that had been the mandate and the ideal of civilised man for three millennia, an ideal so rarely achieved. What flowed from Cordelia was life, deeper, more real than Amanda had ever encountered in her self-absorbed routine with its narrow personal ambitions. It was the love she craved.

The gondola swung slowly earthwards. They came down to the level of rooftops. Black beetles on the ground became cars, pinheads became people. The perspective lengthened horizontally. Amanda had a decision to make. She had purposely not brought her notebook and was glad of it. But another story grew in her head, a bigger story. The trouble was, it was too big for a daily tabloid, whose copy was by definition ephemeral. Should she look for further interviews with these self-styled Christians? She could write up the whole saga into a series of articles and sell it to a magazine. There would be money in that. And she alone was in a position to do it. She was closer to the main actors in the drama than anyone else. She could reveal to the world their inner feelings, their real motives. There was even a book in it. Should she offer to ghost-write the whole story? It could be a bestseller.

But for the first time in her life, presented with a unique

opportunity for a good story, Amanda hesitated. What was the most important thing? The story? Truth? Were they not the same? Cordelia's words haunted her. She needed time to think. But her immediate feeling, as the gondola cruised gently sideways along the landing stage and the doors slid open, was to let the story rest. She had met with something strange and new. Questions remained. But she had found what she had never found before in an interviewee – a friend. Such was the power at work in Cordelia's personality that she no longer appeared as an opponent, or a threat or an accusation. Here was a holiness that did not repel, but attracted. It was warm. It was real affection. It was friendship.

The Eye continued on its measured journey, absorbing the crowds waiting in line at the entrance, disgorging happy groups of people on their descent. Cordelia and Amanda had lunch together and the barriers melted away even more. They were no longer interviewee and reporter, believer and atheist, innocent and streetwise. They were friends. A lot had happened in half an hour.

Before parting, they agreed to meet again, this time with Antony. Antony, the eligible bachelor with the profile of a film star and the figure of a Greek god. It was a measure of the change that was already happening in Amanda that she viewed the chance to meet him as another potential friend, another door opening onto the new world she was discovering; not as a catch, a sexual challenge, a male whom she might bid to entangle in her charms.

CHAPTER 31

Months passed, and the trial came around. It was the last episode of the story, as far as the media were concerned. All the details of the elaborate plot were extracted by the prosecution and reported eagerly by the press: the five months' display of coloured decorations and the secret work on the lion meanwhile – the excavating of a recess under the paving of Trafalgar Square; the introduction of a lifting machine; the lowering of the lion onto it; with a temporary paving supported on girders to cover it. Malcolm, as a borough engineer, had known where to find plans of underground London and had masterminded the operation, though the original idea had been Cordelia's. He had a team of willing volunteers to help, willing to give up countless hours to slow and patient tunnelling, as patient and dedicated as the prisoners who plotted and worked secretly over the long months to effect a breakout from Colditz Castle.

Malcolm, Cordelia and Antony, regarded as the ringleaders of the series of incidents, were made an example of, though such was the massive support of the public and the secret sympathy and admiration of even the prosecuting counsel, that the judge awarded the lightest possible sentence. He could not pass it over entirely, opening the door to anyone to commit outrages on public property with impunity. On the other hand, he well knew their imprisonment would only aid their cause, adding to the publicity and presenting them as martyrs.

The three served a short prison sentence. They let it be known that they rejoiced to think they were in the company of St Paul, John Bunyan, George Fox, William Penn, and thousands of twentieth-century witnesses – Dietrich

Bonhoffer, Martin Niemoller, Corrie ten Boom, Richard Wurmbrandt, Janani Luwum, Brother Yun among them – who had been imprisoned simply for expressing their Christian beliefs. Their trial, sentence and final release made headlines in the national press and short news flashes around the world. The tide of history flowed over the event and the media reverted to things that they judged more important.

An episode in the life of London, a tiny blip in its history of three millennia, faded into the past. Its statues and monuments relapsed into their perennial sleep, adorned only by the droppings of pigeons. And yet a change had been wrought in the thoughts and attitudes of its people. A mark had been made, a small light had shone. A glimpse of true joy, an inkling of a life with purpose and direction, had been revealed; a gentle challenge to the heedless career of the money-getting millions had been made. The positive impact of an almost-forgotten gospel had made a small but significant mark on the ancient city. Here and there, in individuals and little groups, people were re-born to new possibilities. A light had dawned.

Amanda's life was turned around. Partly by good luck, partly by determination and persistence, she had been at the forefront of each incident, often first on the scene and first to get reports back to her paper. With the help of Cordelia she had been in pole position for the climax at the return of the lion. Harry was delighted with her and recommended her for promotion to deputy editor. Still in her mid-twenties, her career was made. Life looked good. But these things seemed less important than they would have done six months before.

Far deeper changes were going on in her inner world. The hard crust of materialism, the ruthless ambition of her kind, the cynicism of her chosen profession were beginning to dissolve. The sequence of colours had had a subtle effect on her mind – as if her life hitherto had been lived in black and white. She was beginning to see for the first time worlds beyond her world. All that she had dismissed with contempt as the tired jargon of an outworn creed was becoming real and alive, more real than the world of streets and shops, the office and the pub; more real than her own petty plans for advancement, the building of a career. Her life was beginning to take on the nature of reality itself.

Without her knowing it, the change in her changed others too. Her work colleagues, Harry, Marcus and the rest, saw the transformation in her, almost before she was aware of it herself. Family, friends, all she came into contact with, saw a new Amanda, and the effect was contagious. She had always prided herself on living life to the full; now she began to realise how little real meaning was contained in the facile phrase. Life in all its fullness was a vista just opening up, an adventure just beginning.

At a time when churches in Britain were not news, Antony Kilbride's church became for a time the most talked-about place in London. More and more people, of all faith backgrounds, were drawn to it. They came for fellowship, for discussion, for counselling, for relaxation, for meditation, for worship. Many came out of pure curiosity. Its mix of unashamed witness and exuberant faith, combined with a genuine love of people as people, was a magnet to many of the lonely and the seeking. Understanding between those of different faiths, passionately held, inched forward. True friendships flourished. Trust deepened and serious debates went on. But with it all a sense of fun, an impish delight in the zany and unexpected, tempered the atmosphere and defused the dangers of becoming strident, fanatical or pompous. Antony saw to that.

The death and rebirth of the lion had a permanent place in the regeneration of British society. It was always remembered as a moment when the tide turned; when demoralised and divided churches began to repent and recognise afresh their true calling; when Christians turned from tolerating Jews and Muslims and began to love them; when the sickening selfishness of materialist greed took a body blow; when the cynical indifference to the world's hunger was exposed; when monetary wealth began to look a little more squalid; when the assumption of rights, the demands for compensation, the habit of complaint and the culture of litigation were questioned. The spirit of the lion, of Aslan the re-born, the lion of the tribe of Judah, the risen and conquering Son, began to regain ground, little by little, in a once-Christian land; and individuals, moved for the first time by a sense of inner need, began to turn to him for guidance and inspiration – not least some of the many thousands who had stood in Trafalgar Square on Monday, 29 August and witnessed the resurrection of the lion.

GLOSSARY

The Met	The (London) Metropolitan Police
Lib Dems	The Liberal Democratic Party, whose colour is yellow
nosh	slang for food
Radox	therapeutic bath essence
Blue Peter	popular daily *TV* programme for children
Notting Hill Carnival	colourful annual festival in West London featuring ethnic minorities
Grand National	annual horse race
The Green Party	political party concerned with the environment
Ribena	popular blackcurrant drink